BOOK 1

Kelly's CHANCE

BRIDES OF LEHIGH CANAL

WANDA E. BRUNSTETTER

New York Times BESTSELLING AUTHOR

BOOK 1

Kelly's CHANCE

BRIDES OF LEHIGH CANAL

BARBOUR

PUBLISHING

© 2004 by Wanda E. Brunstetter

Print ISBN 978-1-63058-164-0

eBook Editions:
Adobe Digital Edition (.epub) 978-1-63058-516-7
Kindle and MobiPocket Edition (.prc) 978-1-63058-517-4

All Scripture quotations are taken from the King James Version of the Bible.

This book is a work of fiction. Names, characters, places, and incidents are either products of the author's imagination or used fictitiously. Any similarity to actual people, organizations, and/or events is purely coincidental.

For more inform... access the author's w... www.wandabrunstetter.c... Wanda E. Brunstetter, please ...llowing Internet address:

Cover design: Müllerhaus Publish...

Published by Barbour Books, an imprint of ...
P.O. Box 719, Uhrichsville, Ohio 44683, www.b...   ...us.net

Our mission is to publish and distribute inspirational prod...
exceptional value and biblical encouragement to the masses.

ecpa Member of the
Evangelical Christian
Publishers Association

Printed in the United States of America.

Dedication/Acknowledgments

To my husband, Richard,
born and raised in Easton, Pennsylvania,
near the Lehigh Canal.
Thanks for your love, support, and research help.

To Char and Mim,
my brother-in-law and sister-in-law.
Thanks for your warm hospitality
as we researched this book.

Chapter 1

Lehigh Valley, Pennsylvania—Spring 1891

───────◆❀◆───────

Kelly McGregor trudged wearily along the towpath, kicking up a cloud of dust with the tips of her worn work boots. A size too small and pinching her toes, they were still preferable to walking barefoot. Besides the fact that the path was dirty, water moccasins from the canal sometimes slithered across the trail. Kelly had been bitten once when she was twelve years old. She shuddered at the memory. . . Papa cutting her foot with a knife, then sucking the venom out. Mama following that up with a poultice of comfrey leaves to take the swelling down, then giving Kelly some willow bark tea for the pain. Ever since that day, Kelly had worn boots while she worked, and even though she could swim quite well, she rarely did so anymore.

As Kelly continued her walk, she glanced over her shoulder and smiled. Sure enough, Herman and Hector were dutifully following, and the rope connected to their harnesses still held taut.

"Good boys," she called to the mules. "Keep on comin'."

Kelly knew most mule drivers walked behind their animals in order to keep them going, but Papa's mules were usually dependable and didn't need much prodding. Herman, the lead mule, was especially obedient and docile. So Kelly walked in front, or sometimes alongside the team, and they followed with rarely a problem.

Herman and Hector had been pulling

Papa's canal boat since Kelly was eight years old, and she'd been leading them for the last nine years. Six days a week, nine months of the year, sometimes eighteen hours a day, they trudged up and down the towpath that ran alongside the Lehigh Navigation System. The waterway, which included the Lehigh Canal and parts of the Lehigh River, was owned by a Quaker named Josiah White. Due to his religious views, he would not allow anyone working for him to labor on the Sabbath. That was fine with Kelly. She needed at least one day of rest.

"If it weren't for the boatmen's children, the canal wouldn't run a day," she mumbled. "Little ones who can't wait to grow up so they can make their own way."

Until two years ago, Kelly's older sister, Sarah, had helped with the mules. Then she ran off with Sam Turner, one of the lock tender's boys who lived along their route. Sarah and Sam had been making eyes at each other for some time, and one day shortly after

Sarah's eighteenth birthday, they ran away together. Several weeks later, Sarah sent the family a letter saying she and Sam were married and living in Phillipsburg, New Jersey. Sam had gotten a job at Warren Soapstone, and Sarah was still looking for work. Kelly and her folks hadn't seen or heard a word from the couple since. Such a shame! She sure did miss that sister of hers.

Kelly moaned as she glanced down at her long, gray cotton skirt, covered with a thick layer of dust. She supposed the sifting dirt was preferable to globs of gritty, slippery mud, which she often encountered in early spring. "Long skirts are such a bother. Sure wish Mama would allow me to wear pants like all the mule boys do."

In the past when the wind was blowing real hard, Kelly's skirt billowed, and she hated that. She'd solved the problem by sewing several small stones into the hemline, weighing her skirt down so the wind couldn't lift it anymore.

Kelly looked over her shoulder again, past the mules. Her gaze came to rest on her father's flat-roofed, nearly square, wooden boat. They were hauling another load of dark, dirty anthracite coal from the town of Mauch Chunk, the pickup spot, on down to Easton, where it would be delivered.

Kelly's thoughts returned to her sister, and a knot rose in her throat. She missed Sarah for more than just her help. Sometimes when they'd walked the mules together, Kelly and Sarah had shared their deepest desires and secret thoughts. Sarah admitted how much she hated life on the canal. She'd made it clear that she would do about anything to get away from Papa and his harsh, stingy ways.

Kelly groaned inwardly. She understood why Sarah had taken off and was sure her older sister had married Sam just so she could get away from the mundane, difficult life on the Lehigh Navigation System. It didn't help any that Kelly and Sarah had been forced to work as mule drivers without earning one penny of their own. Some mule drivers earned as much as a dollar per day, but not Kelly and her sister. All the money they should have made went straight into Papa's pocket, even if Mama and the girls had done more than their share of the work.

In all fairness, Kelly had to admit that, even though he yelled a lot, Papa did take pretty good care of them. He wasn't like some of the canal boatmen, who drank and gambled whenever they had the chance, wasting away their earnings before the month was half over.

Kelly was nearing her eighteenth birthday, and even though she was forced to work without pay, nothing on earth would make her marry someone simply so she could get away. The idea of marriage was like vinegar in her mouth. From what she'd seen in her own folks' lives, getting hitched wasn't so great, anyway. All Mama ever did was work, and all Papa did was take charge of the boat and yell at his family.

Tears burned in Kelly's eyes, but she held

them in check. "Sure wish I could make enough money to support myself. And I don't give a hoot nor a holler 'bout findin' no man to call husband, neither."

Kelly lifted her chin and began to sing softly, "Hunks-a-go pudding and pieces of pie; my mother gave me when I was knee-high. . . . And if you don't believe it, just drop in and see—the hunks-a-go pudding my mother gave me."

The tension in Kelly's neck muscles eased as she began to relax. Singing the silly canaler's tune always made her feel a bit better—especially when she was getting hungry and could have eaten at least three helpings of Mama's hunks-a-go pudding. The fried batter, made with eggs, milk, and flour, went right well with a slab of roast beef. Just thinking about how good it tasted made Kelly's mouth water.

Mama would serve supper when they stopped for the night, but that wouldn't be 'til sundown, several hours from now. When Papa hollered, "Hold up there, girl!" and secured the boat to a tree or near one of the locks, Kelly would have to care for the mules. They always needed to be curried and cleaned, in particular around Herman and Hector's collars where their sweaty hair often came loose. Kelly never took any chances with the mules, for she didn't want either of them to get sores or infections that needed to be treated with medicine.

After the grooming was finished each night, Kelly fed the animals and bedded them down in fresh straw spread along the floor in one of the lock stables or in their special compartment on the boat. Only when all that was done could Kelly wash up and sit down to Mama's hot meal of salt pork and beans or potato and onion soup. Roast beef and hunks-a-go pudding were reserved for a special Sunday dinner when there was more time for cooking.

After supper when all the dishes had been washed, dried, and put away, Kelly read, drew, and sometimes played a game. Mama and Papa amused themselves with an occasional game of checkers, and sometimes they lined up a row of dominoes and competed to see who could acquire the most points. That was fine with Kelly. She much preferred to retire to her bunk in the deck below and draw by candlelight until her eyes became too heavy to focus. Most often she'd sketch something she'd seen along the canal, but many times her charcoal pictures were of things she'd never seen before. Things she'd read about and could only dream of seeing.

On days like today, when Kelly was dog-eared tired and covered from head to toe with dust, she wished for a couple of strong brothers to take her place as mule driver. It was unfortunate for both Kelly and her folks, but Mama wasn't capable of having more children. She'd prayed for it; Kelly had heard her do so many times. The good Lord must have thought two daughters were all Amos and Dorrie McGregor needed. God must have decided Kelly could do the work of two sons. Maybe the Lord believed she should learn to be content with being poor, too.

Contentment. Kelly didn't think she could ever manage to achieve that. Not until she had money in her pockets. She couldn't help but wonder if God cared about her needs at all.

Herman nuzzled the back of Kelly's neck, interrupting her musings and nearly knocking her wide-brimmed straw hat to the ground. She shivered and giggled. "What do ya want, ol' boy? You think I have some carrots for you today? Is that what you're thinkin'?"

The mule answered with a loud bray, and Hector followed suit.

"All right, you two," Kelly said, reaching into her roomy apron pocket. "I'll give ya both a carrot, but you must show your appreciation by pullin' real good for a few more hours." She shook her finger. "And I want ya to do it without one word of complaint."

Another nuzzle with his wet nose, and Kelly knew Herman had agreed to her terms.

Now she needed confirmation from Hector.

———— ❖ ————

Mike Cooper didn't have much use for some of the newfangled things he was being encouraged to sell in his general store, but this pure white soap that actually floated might be a real good seller—especially to the boatmen, who seemed to have a way of losing bars of soap over the side of their vessels. If Mike offered them a product for cleaning that could easily be seen and would bob like a cork instead of sinking to the bottom of the murky canal, he could have a bestseller that would keep his customers coming back and placing orders for "the incredible soap that floats."

Becoming a successful businessman might help him pursue his goal of finding a suitable wife. Ever since Pa had died, leaving him to run the store by himself, Mike had felt a terrible ache in his heart. Ma had gone to heaven a few years before Pa, and his two brothers, Alvin and John, had relocated a short time later, planning to start a fishing business off the coast of New Jersey. That left Mike to keep the store going, but it also left him alone, wishing for a helpmate and a brood of children. Mike prayed for this every day. He felt he was perfectly within God's will to make such a request. After all, in the book of Genesis, God said it wasn't good for a man to be alone, so He created Eve to be a helper and to keep Adam company. At twenty-four years old, Mike thought it was past time he settled down with a mate.

Mike's biggest concern was the fact that there weren't too many unattached ladies living along the canal. Most of the women who shopped at his store were either married or adolescent girls. One young woman—Sarah McGregor—was the exception, but word had it she'd up and run off with the son of a lock tender from up the canal a ways. Sarah had a younger sister, but the last time Mike saw Kelly, she was only a freckle-faced kid in pigtails.

Then there was Betsy Nelson, daughter of the minister who lived in nearby Walnutport and regularly traveled along the canal in hopes of winning folks to the Lord. Betsy wasn't beautiful, but she wasn't as ugly as the muddy waters in Lehigh Canal, either. Of course, Mike wasn't nearly as concerned about a woman's looks as he was with her temperament. Betsy should have been sweet as apple pie, her being a pastor's daughter and all, but she could cut a body right in two with that sharp tongue of hers. Why, he'd never forget the day Betsy raked old Ross Spivey up one side and down the other for spitting out a wad of tobacco in the middle of one of her daddy's sermons. By the time she'd finished with Ross, the poor man was down on his knees, begging forgiveness for being so rude.

Mike grabbed a broom from the storage closet, shook his head, and muttered, "A fellow would have to be hard of hearing or just plain dumb-witted to put up with the likes of Miss Betsy Nelson. It's no wonder she's not married yet."

He pushed the straw broom across the wooden floor, visualizing with each stroke a beautiful, sweet-spirited woman who'd be more than happy to become his wife. After a few seconds, Mike shook his head and murmured, "I'll have to wait, that's all. Wait and keep on praying."

Mike quoted Genesis 2:18, a Bible verse that had become one of his favorites since he'd decided he wanted a wife: " 'And the Lord God said, It is not good that the man should be alone; I will make him an help meet for him.'

"I know the perfect woman is out there somewhere, Lord," he whispered. "All I need is for You to send her my way, and I can take it from there."

CHAPTER 2

❋

Kelly awoke feeling tired and out of sorts. She'd stayed up late the night before, working on another charcoal drawing of an ocean scene with lots of fishing boats on the water. Not that Kelly had ever seen the ocean. Her only experience with water involved the Lehigh, Morris, and Delaware rivers and canals. She'd only seen the ocean in her mind from stories she'd read in books or from the tales of those who had personally been to the coast.

If she could ever figure out a way to earn enough money of her own, Kelly might like to take a trip to the shore. Maybe she would open an art gallery there, to show and sell some of her work. She had seen such a place in the town of Easton, although Papa would never let her go inside. Kelly wondered if her drawings were good enough to sell. If only she could afford to buy a store-bought tablet, along with some oil paints, watercolors, or sticks of charcoal. She was getting tired of making her own pieces of charcoal, using hunks left over in the cooking stove or from campfires along the canal. Kelly let the chunks cool and then whittled them down to the proper size. It wasn't what she would have liked, but at least it allowed her to draw.

Kelly swung her legs over the edge of the bunk and stretched her aching limbs. If a young woman of seventeen could hurt this much from long hours of walking and caring for mules, she could only imagine how older folks must feel. Papa worked plenty hard steering the boat and helping load and unload the coal they hauled, which might account for his crabby attitude. Mama labored from sunup to sunset as well. Besides cooking and cleaning, she always had laundry and mending to do. At times, Mama even steered the boat while Papa rested or took care of chores only he could do. Kelly's mother also helped by watching up ahead and letting Papa know where to direct the boat.

Stifling a yawn, Kelly reached for a plain brown skirt and white, long-sleeved blouse lying on a straight-backed chair near the bed. She glanced around the small cabin and studied her meager furnishings. The room wasn't much bigger than a storage closet, and it was several steps below the main deck. Her only pieces of furniture were the bunk, a small desk, a chair, and the trunk she kept at the foot of her bed.

I wonder what it would be like to have a roomy bedroom in a real house, Kelly mused. The canal boat had been her primary home as far back as she could remember. The only time the lived elsewhere was in the winter, when the canal was drained due to freezing temperatures and couldn't be navigated. Then Kelly's dad worked at one of the factories in Easton. Leaving the few pieces of furniture they owned on their boat, the McGregor family settled into Flannigan's Boardinghouse until the spring thaw came and Papa could resume work on the canal. During the winter months, Kelly and her sister had gone to school when they were younger, but the rest of the year, Mama taught them reading and sums whenever they had a free moment.

Kelly's nose twitched and her stomach rumbled as the distinctive aroma of cooked oatmeal and cinnamon wafted down the stairs, calling her to breakfast. A new day was about to begin, and she would need a hearty meal to help get started.

"We'll be stoppin' by Cooper's General Store this afternoon 'cause we need some supplies," Papa announced when Kelly arrived at the breakfast table. He glanced over at Mama, then at Kelly, his green eyes looking ever so serious. "Don't know when we'll take time out for another supply stop, so if either of you needs anything, you'd better plan on gettin' it today." He slid his fingers across his auburn, handlebar mustache.

"I could use a few more bars of that new-fangled soap I bought last time we came through," Mama spoke up. "It's a wonder to me the way that stuff floats!"

Kelly smiled at her mother's enthusiasm over something as simple as a bar of white soap ~~...~~ guess things like that are important ~~get excited about.~~ ~~doesn't have~~

Kelly ate a spoonful of oatmeal as she studied her mother, a large-boned woman of Italian descent. She had dark brown hair like Kelly's; only Mama didn't wear hers hanging down. She pulled it up into a tight bun at the back of her head. Mama's eyes, the color of chestnuts, were her best feature.

Mama could be real pretty if she was able to

25

have nice, new clothes and keep herself fixed up. Instead, she's growing old before her time—slavin' over a hot stove and scrubbin' clothes in canal water, with only a washboard and a bar of soap that bobs like a cork. Poor Mama!

Papa's chair scraped across the wooden planks as he pulled his wiry frame away from the table. "It's time to get rollin'." He nodded toward Kelly. "Better get them mules ready, girl."

Kelly finished the rest of her breakfast and jumped up. When Papa said it was time to roll, he meant business. For that matter, when Papa said a~~nyth~~ing at all, she knew she'd better listen.

At noon, the McGregors tied their boat to a tree not far from the town of Walnutport and stopped for lunch. Normally they would have eaten a quick bite, then started back up the canal, but today they were heading to Cooper's General Store. After a bowl of vegetable soup and some of Mama's sweet corn bread, they would shop for needed supplies and more food staples.

Kelly welcomed the stop not only because she was hungry, but also because Papa had promised to buy her a new pair of boots. She'd been wearing the same ones for more than a year, and they were much too tight. Besides, the laces were missing, and the soles were worn nearly clear through. Kelly had thought by the time she turned sixteen her feet would have quit growing. But here she was only ten months from her eighteenth birthday, and her long toes were still stretching the boots she wore. At this rate, she feared she'd be wearing a size 9 when her feet finally stopped growing.

Kelly ate hurriedly, anxious to head over to the general store. She hadn't been inside Cooper's in well over a year because she usually chose to wait outside while her folks did the shopping. Today, Kelly planned to check the mules and offer them a bit of feed, then hurry into the store. If she found new boots in short order, there might be enough time to sit on a log and draw awhile. She always found interesting things along the canal—other boats, people fishing, and plenty of waterfowl.

Too bad I can't buy some oil paints or a set of watercolors, Kelly thought as she hooked the mules to a post and began to check them for harness sores, fly bites, or hornet stings. *Guess I should be happy Papa has agreed to buy me new boots, but I'd sure like to have somethin' just for fun once in a while.*

Kelly scratched Hector behind his ear. "If I ever make any money of my own, I might just buy you a big, juicy apple." She patted Herman's neck. "You, too, old boy."

Mike whistled a hymn as he dusted off the candy counter, always a favorite with the children who stopped by. He was running low on horehound drops but still had plenty of licorice, lemon drops, and taffy chews. He knew he'd have to order more of everything soon, since summer was not far off and a lot more little ones would be coming by in hopes of finding something to satisfy their sweet tooth.

Many boats were being pulled up the Lehigh Navigation System already, and it was still early spring. Mike figured by this time next month his store would have even more customers. Last winter, when he'd had plenty of time on his hands, Mike had decided to order some Bibles to either sell or give away. If someone showed an interest and didn't have the money to buy one, he'd gladly offer it to them for free. Anything to see that folks learned about Jesus. Too many of the boatmen were uneducated in spiritual matters, and Mike wanted to do his part to teach them God's ways.

Mike leaned on the glass counter and let his mind wander back to when he was a boy of ten and had first heard about the Lord. Grandma Cooper, a proper Englishwoman, had told him about Jesus. Mike's family had lived with her and Grandpa for several years when Mike's pa was helping out on the farm in upstate New York, where Mike had been born. Ellis Cooper had no mind to stay on the farm, though, and as soon as he had enough money, he moved his wife and three sons to Pennsylvania, where he'd opened the general store along the Lehigh Canal.

Mike's father didn't hold much to religious things. He used to say the Bible was a bunch of stories made up to help folks get through life with some measure of hope.

"There's hope, all right," Mike whispered as he brought his mind back to the present. "And thanks to Grandma's teachings, I'd like to help prove that hope never has to die."

When he heard a familiar creak, Mike glanced at the front door. Enough daydreaming and reflecting on the past. He had customers to satisfy.

As he moved toward the front of the store, Mike's heart slammed into his chest. Coming through the doorway was the most beautiful young woman he'd ever laid eyes on. *Don't* reckon I've seen her before. She must be new. . .just passing through. Maybe she's a passenger on one of the packet boats that hauls tourists. Maybe. . .

Mike blinked a couple of times. He recognized the man and woman entering the store behind the young woman: Amos and Dorrie McGregor. It wasn't until Amos called her by name that Mike realized the beauty was none other than the McGregors' younger daughter, Kelly.

Mike shook his head. It couldn't be. Kelly had pigtails, freckles, and was all arms and legs. This stunning creature had long brown hair that reached clear down to her waist, and from where he stood, not one freckle was visible on her lovely face. She looked his way, and he gasped at the intensity of her dark brown eyes. *A man could lose himself in those eyes. A man could—*

"Howdy, Mike Cooper," Amos said, extending his hand. "How's business these days?"

Mike forced himself to breathe, and with even more resolve, he kept his focus on

Amos and not the man's appealing daughter. "Business is fine, sir." He shook the man's hand. "How are you and the family doing?"

Amos shrugged. "Fair to middlin'. I'd be a sight better if I hadn't hit one of the locks and put a hole in my boat the first week back to work." He gave his handlebar mustache a tug. "In order to get my repairs done, I had to use most of what I made this winter workin' at a shoe factory in Easton."

"Sorry to hear that," Mike said sincerely. He glanced back at Kelly, offering her what he hoped was a friendly smile. "Can this be the same Kelly McGregor who used to come runnin' in here, begging her pa to buy a few lemon drops?"

Kelly's face turned slightly pink as she nodded. "Guess I've grown a bit since you last saw me."

"I'll say!" Mike felt a trickle of sweat roll down his forehead, and he quickly pulled a handkerchief out of his pant's pocket and wiped it away. Kelly McGregor was certainly no child. She was a desirable woman, even if she did have a few layers of dirt on her cotton skirt and wore a tattered straw hat and a pair of boots that looked like they were ready for burial. *Could she be the one I've been waiting for, Lord?*

Mike cleared his throat. "So what can I help you good folks with today?"

Amos nudged his wife. "Now don't be shy, Dorrie. Tell the man what you're needin'. I'll just poke around the store and see what I can still gettin' new boots, right, Papa?"

Her dad nodded. "Yeah, sure. See if Mike has somethin' that'll fit your big feet."

Mike felt sorry for Kelly, whose face was now red as a tomato. She shifted from one foot to the other and never once did she look Mike in the eye.

"I got a new shipment of boots in not long ago," he said quickly, hoping to help her feel

a bit more at ease. "They're right over there."
He pointed to a shelf across the room. "Would
you like me to see if I have any your size?"

Dorrie McGregor spoke up for the first
time. "Why don't you help my husband find
what he's needin'? Me and Kelly can manage
fine on our own."

Mike shrugged. "Whatever you think best."
He offered Kelly the briefest of smiles and then
headed across the room to help her pa.

Kelly didn't know why, but she felt as jittery as
one of the mulan _____
to walk through _____
imagination, or was Mike Cooper _____
her? Ever since they'd entered the store, he'd
seemed to be watching her, and now, while
she stooped down on the floor trying on a pair
of size 9 boots, the man was actually gawking.
*Maybe he's never seen a woman with such big feet.
Probably thinks I should have been born a boy.* Kelly
swallowed hard and forced the threatening tears

34

to stay put. *Truth be told, Papa probably wishes I was a boy.* Most boys were able to work longer and harder than she could. And a boy wasn't as apt to run off with the first person who offered him freedom from canal work, the way Sarah had.

Kelly glanced around the room, feeling an urgency to escape. She stood on shaky legs and forced herself to march around the store a few times in order to see if the boots were going to work out okay. When she was sure they were acceptable, she pulled the price tag off the laces and handed it to Mama. "If ya don't mind, I'd like to wait outside. It's kinda stuffy in here, and since it's such a nice day, maybe I can get in a bit of sketchin' while you and Papa finish your shopping."

Mama nodded, and Kelly scooted quickly out the front door. The sooner she got away from Mike Cooper and those funny looks he kept giving her, the better it would be!

Chapter 3

Kelly's heart was pounding like a hammer as she exited the store, but it nearly stopped beating altogether when Mike Cooper opened the door behind her and called, "Hey, Kelly, don't you want a bag of lemon drops?"

She skidded to a stop on the bottom step, heat flooding her face. She turned slowly to face him. *Why does he have to be so handsome?* Mike's medium-brown hair, parted on the

Kelly's Chance

side and cut just below his ears, curled around his neck like kitten fur. His neatly trimmed mustache jiggled up and down as though he might be hiding a grin. The man's hazel eyes seemed to bore right through her, and Kelly was forced to swallow several times before she could answer his question.

"I. . .uh. . .don't have money to spend on candy just now. New boots are more important than satisfyin' my sweet tooth." She turned away, withdrawing her homemade tablet and a piece of charcoal from the extra-large pocket of her apron.

Kelly was almost to the boat when she felt Mike's hand touch her shoulder. "Hold up there. What's your hurry?" His voice was deep, yet mellow and kind of soothing. Kelly thought she could find pleasure in listening to him talk awhile—if she had a mind to.

"I was plannin' to do a bit of drawing." She stared at the ground, her fingers kneading the folds in her skirt.

Mike moved so he was standing beside her.

Wanda E. Brunstetter

"You're an artist?"

She felt her face flush even more. "I like to draw, but that don't make me an artist."

"It does if you're any good. Can you draw something for me right now?"

She shrugged. "I suppose I could, but don't ya have customers to wait on?"

Mike chuckled. "You've got me there. How about if you draw something while I see what your folks might need? When they're done, I'll come back outside, and you can show me what you've made. How's that sound?"

It sounded fair enough. There was only one problem. Kelly was feeling so flustered, she wasn't sure she could write her own name, much less draw any kind of picture worthy to be shown.

"Guess I can try," she mumbled.

Unexpectedly, he reached out and patted her arm, and she felt a warm tingle shoot all the way up to her neck. Except for Papa's infrequent hugs, no man had ever touched her before. It felt kind of nice, in a funny sort of way. *Could this be why Sarah ran off with Sam Turner? Did Sam look at my sister in a manner that made her mouth go dry and her hands feel all sweaty?* If that's what happened to Sarah, then Kelly knew she had better run as far away from Mike Cooper as she possibly could, for he sure enough was making her feel giddy. She couldn't have that.

She took a few steps back, hoping the distance between them might get her thinking straight again. "See you later," she mumbled.

"Sure thing!" he called as he headed back to the store.

Kelly drew in a deep breath and flopped down on a nearby log. The few minutes she'd spent alone with Mike had rattled her so much she wondered if she still knew how to draw.

In all the times they'd stopped by Cooper's General Store, never once had Mike looked at her the way he had today—like she was someone special, maybe even pretty. *Of course,* she reminded herself, *I usually wait outside, so he hasn't seen me in a while.* The time it took for her folks to shop was a good chance for Kelly to sketch, feed and water the mules, or simply rest her weary bones.

Forcing her thoughts off the handsome storekeeper, Kelly focused her attention on a pair of mallard ducks floating in the canal. The whisper of the wind sang softly as it played with the ends of Kelly's hair. A fat bullfrog posed on the bank nearby. It seemed to be studying a dragonfly hovering above the water. The peaceful scene made Kelly feel one with her surroundings. In no time, she'd filled several pages of her simple drawing pad.

Kelly was pulled from her reverie when Papa and Mama walked up, each carrying a wooden box. She rolled up her artwork and slipped it, along with the hunk of charcoal, inside her pocket. Then she wiped her messy hands on her dusty skirt and jumped to her feet. "Need some help?"

"I could probably use another pair of hands puttin' stuff away in the kitchen," Mama replied.

"Will we be leavin' soon?" Kelly asked,

glancing at Cooper's General Store and wondering if Mike would come back to see her drawings as he'd promised.

"Soon as we get everything loaded," Papa mumbled. "Sure would help if we had a few more hands. Got things done a whole lot quicker when Sarah was here."

Kelly watched her dad climb on board his boat. He'd been traveling the canal ever since he was a small boy. Except for winter when he worked in town, running the boat was Papa's whole life. Though he had a fiery Irish temper, once in a while she caught him whistling, singing some silly tune, or blowing on his mouth harp. Kelly figured he must really enjoy his life on the canal. Too bad he was so cheap and wouldn't hire another person to help out. Most of the canalers had a hired hand to steer the boat while the captain stood at the front and shouted directions.

I wish God had blessed Papa and Mama with a whole passel of boys. Sarah's gone, and I'm hoping to leave someday. Then what will Papa do?

Kelly shrugged. *Guess he'll have to break down and hire a mule driver, 'cause Mama sure can't do everything she does now and drive the mules, too.*

As Kelly followed her mother into the cabin, she set her thoughts aside. They had a long day ahead of them.

Mike hoisted a box to his shoulders and started out the door. He had offered to help Amos McGregor haul his supplies on board the boat. It was the least he could do, considering that Amos had no boys to help. Besides, it would give him a good excuse to talk to Kelly again and see what she'd drawn.

Mike met Amos as the older man was stepping off the boat. "Didn't realize you'd be bringing a box clean out here," Amos commented, tipping his head and offering Mike something akin to a smile.

"I said I'd help, and I thought it would save you a few steps." Mike nodded toward the boat. "Where shall I put this one?"

Amos extended his arms. "Just give it to me."

Taken aback by the man's abruptness, Mike shrugged and handed over the box. Amos turned, mumbled his thanks, and stepped onto the boat.

"Is Kelly on board?" Mike called, surprising himself at his sudden boldness. "I'd like to speak with her a moment."

Kelly's dad whirled around. "What business would ya have with my daughter?"

"She was planning to show me some of her artwork."

Amos shook his head. "Her and them stupid drawings! She's a hard enough worker when it comes to drivin' the mules, but for the life of me, I can't see why she wastes any time scratchin' away on a piece of paper with a stick of dirty, black charcoal."

"We all need an escape from our work, Mr. McGregor," Mike asserted. "Some read, fish, or hunt. Others, like me, choose to whittle." He smiled. "Some, such as your daughter, enjoy drawing."

"Humph! Makes no sense a'tall!" Amos

spun around. "I'll tell Kelly you're out here waitin'. Don't take up too much of her time, though. We're about ready to shove off."

Mike smiled to himself. Maybe Amos wasn't such a tough fellow, after all. He could have said Kelly wasn't receiving any visitors. Or he could have told Mike to take a leap into the canal.

A few minutes later, Kelly showed up. She looked kind of flustered, and he hoped it wasn't on account of him. It could be that her pa had given her a lecture about wasting time sketching. Or maybe he'd made it clear he wanted no one calling on the only daughter he had left. Amos might be afraid his younger child would run off with some fellow the way his older daughter had.

He needn't worry. While I'm clearly attracted to Kelly McGregor, I don't think she's given me more than a second thought today.

Kelly's legs shook as she lifted one foot over the side of the boat and stepped onto dry ground. She could hardly believe Mike Cooper had really come looking for her. Papa was none too happy about it and had told her she wasn't to take much time talking to the young owner of the general store. Kelly figured it was probably because Papa was anxious to be on his way, but from the way her father had said Mike's name, she had to wonder if there might be more to his reason for telling her to hurry. Maybe Papa thought she had eyes for Mike Cooper. Maybe he was afraid she would run off and get married. Well, he needn't worry about that happening!

Mike smiled as Kelly moved toward him. "Did you bring your drawings?"

She averted her gaze. "I only have a few with me, and they're done up on scraps of paper sack so they're probably not so good." She blinked a couple of times. "I got some free newsprint from the *Sunday Call* while we were livin' in Easton, and those pictures have a white background. They're on the boat and might be some better."

"Why not let me be the judge of how good

your pictures are? Can I take a peek at what you've got with you?"

Kelly reached inside her ample apron pocket and retrieved the tablet she'd put together from cut-up pieces of paper sack the size of her Bible. She handed it to Mike and waited for his response.

He studied the drawings, flipping back and forth through the pages and murmuring an occasional "ah. . .so. . .hmm. . ."

She shifted her weight from one foot to the other, wondering what he thought. Did Mike like the sketches? Was he surprised to see her crude tablet? The papers were held in place by strings she'd pushed through with one of Mama's darning needles. Then she'd tied the strings in a knot to hold everything in place. Did Mike's opinion of her artwork and tablet matter? After all, he was nothing to her—just a man who ran a general store along the Lehigh Navigation System.

"These are very good," Mike said. "I especially like the one of the bullfrog ready to pounce on the green dragonfly." He chuckled. "Who won, anyway?"

Kelly blinked. "What?"

"Did the bullfrog get his lunch, or did the dragonfly lure the old toad into the water, then flit away before the croaker knew what happened?"

She grinned. "The dragonfly won."

"That's what I expected."

Kelly pressed a hand to her chest, hoping to still a heart that was beating much too fast. If only Papa or Mama would call her back to the boat. As much as she was enjoying this little chat with Mike, she felt jittery and unsure of herself.

"Have you ever sold any of your work?" Mike asked.

She shook her head. "I doubt anyone would buy a plain old charcoal drawing."

He touched her arm. "There's nothing plain about these, Kelly. I have an inkling some of the folks who travel our canal or live in nearby communities might be willing to pay a fair price for one of your pictures."

Her face heated with embarrassment. "You. . .you really think so?"

He nodded. "The other day, a packet boat came through, transporting a group of people up to Allentown. Two of the men were authors, and they seemed real interested in the landscape and natural beauty growing along our canal."

Kelly sucked in her lower lip as she thought about the prospect. This might be the chance she'd been hoping for. If she could make some money selling a few of her charcoal drawings, maybe she'd have enough to purchase a store-bought drawing table, a good set of watercolors, or perchance some oil paints. Then she could do up some *real* pictures, and if she could sell those. . .

"How about I take two or three of these sketches and see if I can sell them in my store?" Mike asked. "I would keep ten percent and give you the rest. How's that sound?"

Ten percent of the profits for him? Had she heard Mike right? That meant she'd get ninety percent. The offer was more than generous, and it seemed too good to be true.

"Sounds fair, but since I've never sold anything before, I don't know what price to put on the drawings," Kelly said.

"Why not leave that up to me?" Mike winked at her, and she felt like his gentle gaze had caught and held her in a trap. "I've been selling things for several years now, so I think I can figure out a fair price," he said with the voice of assurance.

She nodded. "All right, we have us a deal, but since these pictures aren't really my best, I'll have to go back on the boat and get ya three other pictures."

"That's fine," Mike said as he handed her the drawings.

"The next time we come by your store, I'll ask Papa to stop; then I can check and see if you've sold anything."

Mike reached out his hand. "Partners?"

They shook on it. "Partners."

CHAPTER 4

———❀———

Shaking hands with Mike Cooper had almost been Kelly's undoing. When Mike released her hand, she was trembling and had to clench her fists at her sides in order to keep him from seeing how much his touch affected her.

Mike opened his mouth as if to say something, but he was cut off by a woman's shrill voice.

"Yoo-hoo! Mr. Cooper, I need you!"

Kelly and Mike both turned. Betsy Nelson,

the local preacher's daughter, was heading their way, her long, green skirt swishing this way and that.

Kelly cringed, remembering how overbearing Betsy could be. She didn't simply share the Good News, the way Reverend Nelson did. No, Betsy tried to cram it down folks' throats by insisting they come to Sunday school at the little church in Walnutport, where her father served as pastor.

One time, when Kelly was about seven years old, Betsy had actually told Kelly and her sister, Sarah, that they were going to the devil if they didn't come to Sunday school and learn about Jesus. Papa overheard the conversation and blew up, telling sixteen-year-old Betsy what he thought of her pushy ways. He'd sent her home in tears and told Kelly and Sarah there was no need for either of them to go to church. He said he'd gotten along fine all these years without God, so he didn't think his daughters needed religion.

Mama thought otherwise, and while the

girls were young, she often read them a Bible story before going to bed. When Kelly turned twelve, Mama gave her an old Bible that had belonged to Grandma Minnotti, who'd died and gone to heaven. It was during the reading of the Bible story about Jesus' death on the cross that Kelly had confessed her sins in the quiet of her room one night. She'd felt a sense of hope, realizing Jesus was her personal Savior and would walk with her wherever she went—even up and down the dirty towpath.

What had happened to her childlike faith since then? Had she become discouraged after Sarah ran away with Sam, leaving her with the responsibility of leading the mules? Or had her faith in God slipped because Papa was so mean and wouldn't give Kelly any money for the hard work she did every day?

Kelly's thoughts came to a halt when Betsy Nelson stepped between her and Mike and announced, "I need to buy material for some new kitchen curtains I plan to make."

"Go on up to the store and choose what

you want. I'll be there in a minute," Mike answered with a nod.

Betsy stood grounded to her spot, and Mike motioned toward Kelly. "Betsy, in case you didn't recognize her, this is Kelly McGregor, all grown up."

Kelly felt her face flame, and she opened her mouth to offer a greeting, but Betsy interrupted.

"Sure, I remember you—the skinny little girl in pigtails who refused to go to Sunday school."

Kelly knew that wasn't entirely true, as it had been Papa's decision, not hers. She figured it would be best not to say anything, however.

Betsy squinted her gray blue eyes and reached up to pat the tight bun she wore at the back of her head. Kelly wondered if the young woman ever allowed her dingy blond hair to hang down her back. Or did the prim and proper preacher's daughter even sleep with her hair pulled back so tightly her cheeks looked drawn?

"I was hoping you would help me choose the material," Betsy said, offering Mike a pinched-looking smile.

Mike fingered his mustache and rocked back on his heels. Kelly thought he looked uncomfortable. "I'm kind of busy right now," he said, nodding at Kelly.

"It's all right," she was quick to say. "Papa's about ready to go, and I think we've finished with our business."

"But you haven't given me any pictures," Mike reminded her.

"Oh. . .oh, you're right." Kelly's voice wavered when she spoke. She was feeling more flustered by the minute.

"Kelly, you got them mules ready yet?" Papa shouted from the bow of the boat.

Kelly turned to her father and called, "In a minute, Papa." She faced Mike again. "I'll be right back with the drawings." She whirled around, sprinted toward the boat, and leaped over the side, nearly catching her long skirt in the process.

A few minutes later, Kelly came back, carrying three drawings done on newsprint and neatly pressed between two pieces of cardboard. Two were of children fishing along the canal, and the third was a picture of Hector and Herman standing in the middle of the towpath. She handed them to Mike. "I'll have more to show you the next time we stop by."

Mike lifted the top piece of cardboard and studied the drawings. "Nicely done, Kelly. Very nice."

Heat rushed to Kelly's face. "Thanks. I hope the others will be as good."

"I don't see why they wouldn't be." Mike held up the picture of Kelly's mules. "Look, Betsy. See what Kelly's drawn."

"Uh-huh. Nice." Betsy barely took notice as she grabbed hold of Mike's arm. "Can we go see about that material now?"

"I guess so." Mike turned to Kelly. "See you in a few days."

She nodded. "If Papa decides to stop. If not, then soon, I hope."

"Kelly McGregor!" Papa's voice had grown even louder, and Kelly knew he was running out of patience.

"Ready in a minute," she hollered back. "See you, Mike. See you, Betsy." Kelly grabbed hold of the towline and hurried off toward the mules waiting patiently under a maple tree. A few minutes later, she was trudging up the towpath, wishing she could have visited with Mike a bit longer.

Kelly glanced over her shoulder and saw Betsy hanging on to Mike's arm. A pang of jealousy stabbed her heart, but she couldn't explain it. She had no claims on Mike Cooper, nor did she wish to have any. Betsy Nelson was more than welcome to the storekeeper.

Mike headed for the store, wishing it were Kelly and not Betsy clinging to his arm. As he reached the front door, he glanced over his shoulder and saw the McGregors' canal boat disappear around the bend. He'd wanted to

spend more time with Kelly, but Betsy's inter-
ruption had stolen what precious moments
they might have had.

As he stepped into the store, Mike shot a
quick prayer heavenward. *Is Kelly the one, Lord?
Might she make me a good wife?*

"Mr. Cooper, are you listening to me?"
Betsy gave his shirtsleeve a good tug.

Mike refocused his thoughts and turned to
look at Betsy, still clinging to his arm.

"The material's on that shelf, and please feel
free to call me Mike." He pulled his arm free
and pointed to the wall along the left side of his
store. "Give me a minute to put Kelly's drawings
in a safe place, and I'll join you over there."

Mike could see by the pucker of Betsy's lips
that she wasn't happy, but she headed in the
direction he had pointed.

Did Betsy think he would drop everything
just because she wanted his opinion on the
material she wished to buy? Mike doubted his
advice counted for much. He knew little about
kitchen curtains. His mother had decorated

the house he lived in, which was connected to the back of the store. Since Ma's death, he hadn't given much thought to her choice of colors, fabric, or even furniture. If it had been good enough for Ma and Pa, then it was good enough for him.

Mike placed Kelly's drawings on a shelf under the counter and headed across the room to where Betsy stood holding a bolt of yellow and white calico material.

She smiled at him. "What do you think of this color?"

He shrugged. "Guess it would work fine."

For the next half hour, Mike looked at bolts of material, nodded his head, and tried to show an interest in Betsy's curtain-making project. He felt relieved when another customer entered the store, but much to his disappointment, Betsy was still looking at material when he finished up with Hank Summers' order.

"Have you made a decision yet?" Mike called to Betsy from where he stood behind the counter.

"I suppose the yellow and white calico will work best." Betsy marched across the room and plunked the bolt of material on the wooden counter. "I'll take ten yards."

Ten yards? Mike thought Betsy was only making curtains for the kitchen, not every window in the house. *Guess women are prone to changing their minds.*

Betsy grinned at him and fluttered her pale eyelashes. "I'm thinking of making a dress from the leftover material, and I want to be sure I have plenty. Do you think this color will look good on me?"

Mike groaned inwardly. He didn't want to offend the preacher's daughter, so he merely smiled and nodded in response.

As soon as Betsy left the store, Mike pulled Kelly's pictures from under the counter, took a seat on his wooden stool, and studied the charcoal drawings.

Kelly McGregor had talent; there was no doubt about it. The question was, would he be able to sell her artwork?

CHAPTER 5

Over the next couple of days, Kelly daydreamed a lot while she walked the towpath. Was it possible that Mike Cooper might be able to sell some of her drawings? Were they as good as he'd said, or had Mike been trying to be polite when he told Kelly she had talent?

"Sure wish he wasn't so handsome," Kelly muttered as she neared the changing bridge where she and the mules would cross to the other side of the canal. A vision of Mike's face crept into her mind, and she began to sing her favorite canal song, hoping to block out all thoughts of the storekeeper.

"Hunks-a-go pudding and pieces of pie; my mother gave me when I was knee-high. . . . And if you don't believe it, just drop in and see—the hunks-a-go pudding my mother gave me."

Kelly found herself thinking about food and how good supper would taste when they stopped for the night. Mama had bought a hunk of dried beef at Mike Cooper's store, so they would be having savory stew later on.

It was time to get the mules ready to cross over to the towpath on the other side of the canal. Soon they were going up and over the changing bridge, as Kelly lifted the tow-rope over the railing. Obediently, Hector and Herman followed. In no time, they were on the other side, and Papa was able to steer his boat farther down the canal.

Kelly was relieved the towline hadn't become snagged. Whenever that happened, they were held up while Papa fixed things.

Then he was angry the rest of the day because they'd lost precious time. Every load of anthracite coal was important, and payment was made only when it was delivered to the city of Easton, where it was weighed and unloaded. The trip back up the navigation system to Mauch Chunk was with an empty boat, and Papa never wanted to waste a single moment.

Today they were heading to Easton and would arrive by late afternoon if all went well. Kelly knew there was no way Papa would agree to stop by Cooper's General Store on the way to deliver their coal, but coming back again, he might.

Maybe we'll get there early enough so I'll have time to get some drawing done, Kelly told herself. If there was any possibility of Mike selling her artwork, she needed to have more pictures ready to give him.

Kelly didn't realize she'd stopped walking until she felt Hector's wet nose nudge the back of her neck. She whirled around. "Hey there, boy. Are ya that anxious to get to Easton?"

The mule snorted in response, and she laughed and reached out to stroke him behind the ear. Not to be left out, Herman bumped her hand.

"All right, Herman the Determined, I'll give you some attention, too." Kelly stroked the other mule's ear for a few seconds, and then she clicked her tongue. "Now giddy-up, you two. There's no more time to dawdle. Papa will be worse than a snappin' turtle if we make him late tonight."

The day wore on, and every few miles the boat came to another lock where they would wait while it filled with water to match the level of the canal. Then they entered the lock, and the gates enclosed the boat in a damp, wooden receptacle. Right ahead, the water came sizzling and streaming down from above, and gradually the boat would rise again, finally coming to a respectable elevation. The gates swung open, Kelly hooked the mules back to the towrope, and they resumed their voyage.

Ahead was another lock, and Papa blew on

his conch shell, letting the lock tender know he was coming. When they approached the lock, Kelly saw another boat ahead of them. They would have to wait their turn.

Suddenly, a third boat came alongside Papa's. "Move outta my way!" the captain shouted. "I'm runnin' behind schedule and should've had this load delivered by now."

"I was here first," Papa hollered in response. "You'll have to wait your turn."

"Oh, yeah? Who's gonna make me?" The burly looking man with a long, full beard shook his fist at Papa.

Standing on the bank next to the mules, Kelly watched as Mama stepped up beside Papa. She touched his arm and leaned close to Papa's ear. Kelly was sure Mama was trying to get Papa calmed down, like she always did whenever he got riled.

Kelly took a few steps closer to the canal and strained to hear what Mama was saying.

"Don't tell me what to do, woman!" Papa yelled as he leaned over the side of his boat.

The other craft was right alongside him, and the driver of the mules pulling that boat stood next to Kelly.

The young boy, not much more than twelve or thirteen years old, gave Kelly a wide grin. His teeth were yellow and stained. Probably from smoking or chewing tobacco, Kelly figured. "Looks like my pa is gonna beat the stuffin's outa your old man," he taunted.

Kelly glanced back at the two boat captains. They were face-to-face, each leaning as far over the rails as possible. She sent up a quick prayer. *Not this time, Lord. Please help Papa calm down.*

"Move aside, or I'm comin' over there to clean your clock," the burly man bellowed.

"Amos, please!" Mama begged as she gripped Papa's arm again. "Just let the man pass through the lock first. This ain't worth gettin' into a skirmish over."

Papa shot the man a look of contempt and grabbed hold of the tiller in order to steer the boat. "I'll let it go this time, but you'd better never try to ace me out again."

Kelly breathed a sigh of relief as Papa steered the boat aside and the other vessel passed through the lock. She'd seen her hot-tempered father use his fists to settle many disagreements in the past. It was always humiliating, and what did it prove—that Papa was tougher, meaner, or more aggressive than someone else? As far as Kelly could tell, nothing good had ever come from any of Papa's fistfights. He was a hotheaded Irishman who'd grown up on the water. His dad had been one of the men who'd helped dig the Lehigh Canal, and Papa had said many times that he'd seen or been part of a good many fights throughout his growing-up days. If only he would give his heart to Jesus and confess his sins, the way Kelly and Mama had done.

Herman nuzzled Kelly's shoulder, and she turned to face her mule friends. *If God really loves me, then why doesn't He change Papa's heart?*

Kelly's Chance

Mike had been busier than usual the last couple days, and that was good. It kept him from thinking too much about Kelly McGregor. How soon would she and her family stop at his store again? Could he manage to sell any of her drawings before they came? Was Kelly the least bit interested in him? All these thoughts tumbled around in Mike's head whenever he had a free moment to look at Kelly's artwork, which he'd displayed on one wall of the store. The young woman had been gifted with a talent so great that even a simple, homemade charcoal drawing looked like an intricate work of art. At least Mike thought it did. He just hoped some of his customers would agree and decide to buy one of Kelly's pictures.

As Mike wiped off the glass on the candy counter, where little children had left fingerprint smudges, a vision of Kelly came to mind. With her long, dark hair hanging freely down her back, and those huge brown eyes reminding him of a baby deer, she was sure easy to look at. Nothing like Betsy Nelson, the preacher's daughter, who had a birdlike nose, squinty gray blue eyes, and a prim-and-proper bun for her dingy blond hair.

Kelly's personality seemed different, too. She wasn't pushy and opinionated, the way Betsy was. Kelly, though a bit shy, seemed to have a zest for life that showed itself in her drawings. She was a hard worker, too—trudging up and down the towpath six days a week, from sunup to sunset. Mike was well aware of the way the canal boatmen pushed to get their loads picked up and delivered. The responsibility put upon the mule drivers was heavy, yet it was often delegated to women and children.

I wonder if Amos McGregor appreciates his daughter and pays her well enough. Mike doubted it, seeing the way the man barked orders at Kelly. And why, if she was paid a decent wage, would Kelly be using crude sticks of charcoal instead of store-bought paints or pencils, not to mention her homemade tablet?

Mike's thoughts were halted when the front door of his store opened and banged shut.

"Good morning, Mike Cooper," Preacher Nelson said as he sauntered into the room.

"Mornin'," Mike answered with a smile and a nod.

"How's business?"

"Been kind of busy the last couple of days. Now that the weather's warmed and the canal is full of water again, the boatmen are back in full swing."

The preacher raked his long fingers through the ends of his curly, dark hair. His gray blue eyes were small and beady, like his daughter's. "You still keeping the same hours?" the man questioned.

Mike nodded. "Yep. . .Monday to Saturday, nine o'clock in the morning till six at night."

Hiram Nelson smiled, revealing a prominent dimple in his clean-shaven chin. "Sure glad to hear you're still closing the store on Sundays."

Mike moved over to the wooden counter where he waited on customers. "Sunday's a day of rest."

"That's how God wants it, but there's sure a lot of folks who think otherwise."

Not knowing what else to say, Mike merely shrugged. "Anything I can help you with, Reverend Nelson?"

The older man leaned on the edge of the counter. "Actually, there is."

"What are you in need of?"

"You."

"Me?"

The preacher's head bobbed up and down. "This Friday's my daughter's twenty-sixth birthday, and I thought it would be nice for Betsy if someone her age joined us for supper." He chuckled. "She sees enough of her old papa, and since her mama died a few years ago, Betsy's been kind of lonely."

Mike was tempted to remind the preacher that his daughter was two years older than he but decided not to mention their age difference—or the fact that most women Betsy's age were already married and raising a family. "Isn't there someone from your church you could invite?" he asked.

Pastor Nelson's face turned slightly red. "It's you Betsy thought of when she said she'd like to have a guest on her birthday." He tapped the edge of the counter.

Mike wasn't sure how to respond. Was it possible that Betsy Nelson was romantically interested in him? If so, he had to figure out a way to discourage her.

"So, what do you say, son? Will you come to supper on Friday evening?"

Remembering that the Nelsons' home was next to the church and several miles away, Mike knew he would have to close the store early in order to make it in time for supper. This would be the excuse he needed to decline the invitation. Besides, what if the McGregors came by while he was gone? He didn't want to miss an opportunity to see Kelly again.

"I–I'm afraid I can't make it," Mike said.

The preacher pursed his lips. "Why not? You got other plans?"

Mike shook his head. "Not exactly, but I'd have to close the store early."

Reverend Nelson held up his hand. "No need for that, son. We'll have a late supper. How's seven o'clock sound?"

"Well, I—"

"I won't take no for an answer, so you may as well say you'll come. Betsy would be impossible to live with if I came home and told her you'd turned down my invitation."

Mike didn't want to hurt Betsy's feelings, and the thought of eating someone else's cooking did have some appeal. "Okay," he finally conceded. "Tell Betsy I'll be there."

CHAPTER 6

❋

Kelly hummed to herself as she kicked the stones beneath her feet. They had made it to Easton by six o'clock last night, and after they dropped off their load of coal and ate supper, she'd had a few hours to spend in her room, working on her drawings.

Now they were heading back to Mauch Chunk for another load. By five or six o'clock they should be passing Mike Cooper's store. Kelly hoped she could talk Papa into stopping, for she had three more drawings she wanted to give Mike. One was of a canal boat going through the locks, another of an elderly boatman standing at the bow of his boat playing a fiddle, and the third was of the skyline of Easton, with its many tall buildings.

Kelly was pretty sure her pictures were well done, although she knew they could have been better if they'd been drawn on better paper, in color instead of black and white.

She stopped humming. *Someday I hope to have enough money to buy all kinds of paints and fancy paper.* Even as the words popped into her mind, Kelly wondered if they could ever come true. Unless Papa changed his mind about paying her wages, she might never earn any money of her own. Maybe her dream of owning an art gallery wasn't possible.

"At least I can keep on drawing," she mumbled. "Nobody can take that away from me."

Kelly's stomach rumbled, reminding her it was almost noon. Since they had no load, they would be stopping to eat soon. If Papa was hurrying to get to Easton with a boatload of coal, Kelly might be forced to eat a hunk of bread or some fruit and keep on walking. Today, Mama was fixing a pot of vegetable and bean soup. Kelly could smell the delicious aroma as it wafted across the space between the boat and towpath.

A short while later, Kelly was on board the boat, sitting at the small wooden table. A bowl of steaming soup had been placed in front of her, a chunk of rye bread to her left, and her drawing pad was on the right. She'd decided to sketch a bit while her soup cooled.

Kelly had just picked up her piece of charcoal to begin drawing when Papa sat down across from her. "You ain't got time to dawdle. Get your lunch eaten and go tend to the mules."

Tears stung Kelly's eyes. She should be used to the way her dad shot orders, but his harsh tone and angry scowl always upset her.

"My soup's too hot to eat yet," she said. "I thought I might get some drawin' done while

I wait for it to cool."

Papa snorted. "Humph! Fiddlin' with a dirty stick of charcoal is a waste of time!" He grabbed the loaf of bread from the wooden bowl in the center of the table and tore off a piece. Then he dipped the bread into his bowl of soup and popped it into his mouth.

Kelly wasn't sure how she should respond to his grumbling, so she leaned over and blew on her soup instead of saying anything.

Mama, who was dishing up her own bowl of soup at the stove, spoke up. "I don't see what harm there'd be in the girl drawin' while her soup cools, Amos."

Papa slammed his fist down on the table so hard Kelly's piece of bread flew up and landed on the floor. "If I want your opinion, Dorrie, I'll ask for it!"

Kelly gulped. She hated it when Papa yelled at Mama. It wasn't right, but she didn't know what she could do about it. Only God could change Papa's heart, and she was growing weary of praying for such.

"Well, what are ya sittin' there lolly-gaggin' for?" Papa bellowed. "Start eatin', or I'm gonna pitch your writing tablet into the stove."

Kelly grabbed her spoon. No way could she let her dad carry through with his threat. She'd eat all her soup in a hurry, even if she burned her tongue in the process.

Awhile later, she was back on the towpath. She'd given the mules some oats in their feed-bags, and they were munching away as they plodded dutifully along. Kelly knew they were making good time, and they'd probably pass Mike Cooper's sometime early this evening. She'd hoped to ask Papa about stopping by the store, but he'd been so cross during lunch, she'd lost her nerve.

Besides, what reason would she give for stopping? She sure couldn't tell her dad she wanted to make a few more drawings so Mike could try to sell them. Papa had made it clear the way he felt about Kelly wasting time on her artwork. If she told him her plans, Papa might

Wanda E. Brunstetter

make good on his threat and pitch her tablet into the stove.

"If he ever does that, I'll make another one or find some old pieces of cardboard to draw on," Kelly fumed.

A young boy about eight years old crossed Kelly's path. He carried a fishing pole in one hand and a metal bucket in the other. The child stopped on the path and looked at Kelly as though she was daft. Had he overheard her talking to herself?

Kelly stopped walking. "Goin' fishin'?" *What a dumb question. Of course he's goin' fishin'. Why else would he be carryin' a pole?*

The freckle-faced, red-haired lad offered Kelly a huge grin, revealing a missing front tooth. "Thought I'd try to catch myself a few catfish. They was bitin' real good yesterday afternoon."

"You live around here?" Kelly questioned.

"Yep. Up the canal a ways."

Kelly's forehead wrinkled. She didn't remember seeing the boy before, and she wondered why he wasn't in school. The youngster's overalls were torn and dirty, and when Kelly glanced down at his bare feet, she shuddered. It was too cold yet to be going without shoes. Maybe the child was so poor his folks couldn't afford to buy him any decent footwear.

"My pap's workin' up at Mauch Chunk, loadin' coal," the boy said before Kelly could voice any questions.

"But I thought you said you lived nearby."

He nodded. "For the last couple months we've been livin' in an old shanty halfway up the canal." He frowned. "Don't see Pap much these days."

"Do you live with your mother?" Kelly asked.

The boy offered her another toothless grin. "Me, Ma, and little Ted. He's my baby brother. Pap was outa work for a spell, but things will be better now that he's got a job loadin' dirty coal."

Kelly's heart went out to the young child, since she could relate to being poor. Of course,

Papa had always worked, and they'd never done without the basic necessities. Still, she had no money of her own.

"Kelly McGregor, why have you stopped?"

Kelly whirled around at the sound of her dad's angry-sounding voice. He was leaning over the side of the boat, shaking his fist at her.

"Sorry, Papa," she hollered back. "Nice chattin' with you," Kelly said to the child. "Hope you catch plenty of fish today." She gave the boy a quick wave and started off.

As Kelly led her mules down the rutted path, she found herself envying the freckle-faced boy with the holes in his britches. At least he wasn't being forced to work all day.

Mike pulled a pocket watch from his pant's pocket. It was almost six o'clock. He needed to close up the store and head on over to the preacher's place for supper. All day long he'd hoped the McGregors would stop by, but they hadn't, and he'd seen no sign of their boat.

Of course, they could have gone by without him seeing, as there were many times throughout the day when he'd been busy with customers. As tempting as it had been, Mike knew he couldn't stand at the window all day and watch for Amos McGregor's canal boat. He had a store to run, and that took precedence over daydreaming about Kelly or watching for her dad's boat to come around the bend.

Mike put the CLOSED sign in the store window and grabbed his jacket from a wall peg near the door. He was almost ready to leave when he remembered that tonight was Betsy's birthday and he should take her a gift.

He glanced around the store, looking for something appropriate. Mike noticed the stack of Bibles he had displayed on a shelf near the front of his store. He'd given plenty of them away, but he guessed Betsy, being a preacher's daughter, probably had at least one Bible in her possession.

As he continued to survey his goods, Mike's gaze came to rest on Kelly's drawings, tacked up on one wall. What better gift than something made by one of the locals? He chose the picture that showed two children fishing along the canal. He thought Betsy would like it. This would be Kelly's first sale, and he would give her the money she had coming as soon as he saw her again.

Since it was a pleasant spring evening with no sign of rain, Mike decided to walk to the Nelsons' rather than ride his horse or hitch up the buggy. He scanned the canal, looking for any sign of the McGregors' boat, but the only movement on the water was a pair of mallard ducks.

Mike filled his lungs with fresh air as he trudged off toward Walnutport. Sometime later, he arrived at the Nelsons' front door.

Betsy greeted him, looking prim and proper in a crisp white blouse and long blue skirt. Her hair was pulled into its usual tight bun at the back of her head.

"Come in, Mr. Cooper—I mean, Mike," she said sweetly. "Supper is ready, so let me take your coat."

KELLY'S CHANCE

Mike stepped inside the small, cozy parsonage and slipped off his jacket. He was about to hand it to Betsy when he remembered the picture he'd rolled up and put inside his pocket. He retrieved it and handed the drawing to Betsy. "Happy birthday."

Betsy smiled and unrolled the picture. She studied it a few seconds, and her forehead creased as she squinted her eyes. "This isn't one of those drawings young Kelly McGregor drew, is it?"

Mike nodded. "I thought you might like it, seeing as how there are children in the picture."

Her frown deepened. "What makes you think I have a fondness for children?"

"Well, I. . .that is, doesn't everyone have a soft spot for little ones?" Mike thought about his desire to have a large family, and he remembered reading how Jesus had taken time to visit with children. It only seemed natural for a preacher's daughter to like kids.

Betsy scrunched up her nose, as though

Wanda E. Brunstetter

some foul odor had permeated the room. "Children are sometimes hard to handle, and I don't envy anyone who's a parent." She batted her eyelashes a few times. "I get along better with adults."

Mike wondered if there was something in Betsy's eye. Or maybe she had trouble seeing and needed a pair of spectacles.

"Do you like Kelly's charcoal drawing or not?" he asked.

Betsy glanced at the picture in her hand. "I'll find a place for it, since you were thoughtful enough to bring me a present."

Mike drew in a deep breath and followed Betsy into the next room, where a table was set for three. Preacher Nelson stood in front of the fireplace, and he smiled at Mike.

"Good to see you, son. Glad you could make it tonight."

Mike nodded and forced a smile in return. He had a feeling it was going to be a long evening, and he could hardly wait for it to come to an end.

CHAPTER 7

———◆❀◆———

Kelly plodded along the towpath, tired from another long day, and feeling frustrated because they'd passed Mike's store without stopping. It was getting dark by the time they got to that section of the navigation system, and she hadn't seen any lights in the store windows. Maybe Mike was closed for the day.

It had been less than a week since Kelly had left three of her drawings with him. Chances were none of them had sold yet. By the time they did stop at Cooper's General Store, Kelly thought she would have a few more drawings to give Mike, and hopefully he'd have good news about the ones he was trying to sell. In the meantime, Kelly knew she needed to be patient.

"Patient and determined," she muttered into the night air. The moon was full, and Kelly could see some distance ahead. They were coming to another lock, and Papa was already blowing on his conch shell to announce their arrival to the lock tender.

Kelly looked forward to each lock they went through. It gave her a chance to rest, tend to the mules, or draw.

She patted her apron pocket. *That's why I keep my tablet and a hunk of charcoal with me most of the time.*

Tonight, however, there were no boats ahead of them, and they went through the lock rather quickly. Kelly wasn't disappointed. It was too dark to draw anyway, and getting through the lock meant they would soon be on their way.

Kelly was hungry and tired. She could hardly wait to stop for the night. But she didn't smell the usual aroma of food coming from the boat. It made her wonder if Mama was tired and had decided to serve a cold meal. Maybe cheese and bread, with a piece of fruit or some carrot sticks. Anything would taste good.

When Kelly thought she'd die of hunger and couldn't take another step, Papa hollered for her to stop. With her dad's help, Kelly loaded the mules onto the boat, where they would be bedded down in the enclosed area reserved for them. If they'd been at a place where they could have stabled the mules, they wouldn't have to go through this procedure.

Kelly stretched her limbs with a weary sigh. "What's Mama got planned for supper, do ya know?"

Papa shook his head. "Your mama ain't feelin' well, and she's taken to her bed. You'll have to see about supper tonight."

Kelly felt immediate concern. "Mama's sick? What's wrong, and why didn't you tell me sooner?"

Papa shrugged. "Saw no need."

"But I could've come aboard and started supper. Maybe seen if there was somethin' I could do to make Mama more comfortable."

Papa grunted. "It's best you kept on walkin'. I don't wanna be late picking up my load of coal in Mauch Chunk tomorrow."

Kelly stared down at her clenched hands as anger churned in her stomach. All Papa cared about was hauling coal and making money he never shared. Didn't he give a hoot that Mama was sick in bed?

Feeling as though she carried the weight of the world on her shoulders, Kelly headed for their small kitchen. She would get some soup heating on the stove, then go below to see how Mama was doing.

A short time later, Kelly and her dad sat at the kitchen table, eating soup and bread—

leftovers from their afternoon meal. Kelly had checked on her mother and found her sleeping. She didn't have the heart to wake her, so she tiptoed out of her parents' cubicle with the intention of offering Mama a bowl of soup later on.

"You'd better get to sleep right after ya clean up the dishes," Papa said. "I'm planning to head out at the first light of day tomorrow mornin'." He wiped his mouth on the edge of his shirtsleeve. "If your mama's still feelin' poorly, you'll need to get breakfast."

Kelly watched the flame flicker from the candle in the center of the table. More chores to do. Just what she didn't need. She'd better pray extra hard for Mama tonight.

Mike had never been so glad to see his humble home. The time he'd spent at the Nelsons' had left him feeling irritable and exhausted. Didn't Betsy ever stop talking or batting her eyelashes? Reverend Nelson had acted a bit strange all evening, too. He kept dropping hints about his daughter needing a God-fearing husband, and he'd even asked Mike to sit on the sofa beside Betsy as they drank their coffee after dinner. Maybe the preacher was trying to link Mike up with his daughter, but it wasn't going to work. Mike had other ideas about who was the right woman for him.

Mike hung his jacket on a wall peg near the door, sank into an overstuffed chair by the stone fireplace, and looked around the room. He really did need someone to help fill his lonely evening hours. He'd been praying for a wife for some time now, but surely Betsy Nelson wasn't the one God had in mind for him. The woman got on his nerves, with her constant jabbering and opinionated remarks.

"It doesn't seem as if she likes children, either," Mike murmured. He didn't see any way he could be happily married to a woman who didn't share his desire for a family. Mike saw children as a gift from God, not a nuisance. He'd had customers come into his store who'd done nothing but yell at their kids, shouting orders or scolding them for every little thing.

Mike's thoughts went immediately to Kelly McGregor. Did she like children? Would Kelly make a good wife? Was she a believer in Christ? Mike knew so little about the young woman. The only thing he was sure of was that he was attracted to her.

I need to figure out some way for us to become better acquainted. With the McGregors' canal boat coming by every few days, there ought to be a chance to see Kelly more and get to know her.

Mike closed his eyes, and a few minutes later he fell asleep, dreaming about Kelly McGregor.

Kelly stretched her aching limbs and forced herself to sit up. Inky darkness enveloped her room, but Papa was hollering at her to get up. She needed to see if Mama was still ailing, and if so, fix some breakfast. Then she'd have to feed the mules, lead them off the boat, and get ready to head for Mauch Chunk. She hadn't slept well the night before, and she'd had several dreams—one that involved Mike Cooper.

Why do I think about him so often? Kelly fumed. *Probably because he has my drawings, and I'm anxious to see if he's sold any. Yep, that's all there is to it—nothin' more.*

After Kelly washed up and got dressed, she rolled up her finished drawings and placed them inside her apron pocket, just in case they made a stop at Cooper's store today. Then she tiptoed over to her folks' room to check on Mama.

Her mother was awake, but she looked terrible. Dark circles lay beneath her eyes, her skin was pasty white, and her forehead glistened with sweat.

"How are ya feelin' this mornin'?" Kelly whispered.

Mama lifted her head off the pillow and offered Kelly a weak smile. "I'll be back on my feet in no time a'tall. It's just a sore throat, and my body aches some, too."

Kelly adjusted the patchwork quilt covering her mother's bed. "I'll bring you a cup of hot tea and a bowl of cornmeal mush as soon as I get Papa fed. He might be less crabby if his belly is full."

Mama nodded, coughed, and relaxed against the pillow. "I'm sorry you're havin' to do more chores than usual. If Sarah were still here, your load would be a bit lighter."

Kelly shrugged. She didn't want to think about her runaway sister. "I'll manage. You just get well." She patted the quilt where Mama's feet were hidden. "I'll be back soon."

A short while later, Kelly was in the kitchen preparing breakfast.

"What about lunch and supper?" she asked her dad when she handed him a bowl of mush.

His forehead wrinkled. "What about it?"

"If I'm gonna be leadin' the mules all day, and Mama's still sick in bed—"

Papa grunted and pulled on the end of his mustache. "Guess that means I'll be stuck with the cookin'."

"But how will you do that, watch up ahead, and steer the boat, too?" she questioned.

"I'll manage somehow. Don't guess I've got much other choice." He snorted. "If that renegade sister of yours hadn't run off with Sam Turner, we wouldn't be shorthanded right now."

Kelly drew in a deep breath, feeling a bit put out with her sister, too.

Things seemed to go from bad to worse as the day progressed. Kelly kept an eye on the boat, and a couple times she spotted her dad racing back and forth between the woodstove sitting on the open deck and the stern of the boat. He would lift the pot lid and take a look at the beans he was cooking, run back to the stern and give the tiller a twist, and do it all over again. Kelly wondered if he might collapse or run the boat aground from all that rushing around.

When it came time for lunch, Papa gulped down a hasty meal, leaped from the boat to the towpath, and took over leading the mules so Kelly could eat. She did all right getting into the boat, but when she jumped over the side again, she missed her mark and landed in the canal with a splash.

Now she was walking the towpath in a sopping wet skirt that stuck to her legs like a tick on a mule. She'd been forced to remove her boots because they were waterlogged, and she sure hoped no snakes came slithering across the path and nailed her bare feet.

To make matters worse, the drawings she'd put in her pocket that morning had gotten ruined when she fell in the water. Now she had nothing to give Mike if she saw him today.

The only bright spot in Kelly's day was when Papa told her they would be stopping by Cooper's General Store later on. He wanted to see if Mike had any cough syrup in stock. Papa thought it might make Mama sleep better if they could get her cough calmed down. Stopping at the store would be good for Mama as well as Kelly. She hoped her dress would be dry by the time they got there.

CHAPTER 8

For the past couple of days, Mike had tried unsuccessfully to sell some of Kelly's drawings. "Isn't there anyone in the area who can see her talent and needs something special to give as a gift?" he muttered as he studied the two remaining pictures displayed on the wall of his store. Was it possible that Kelly wasn't as talented as Mike thought? Maybe folks were put off by the simplicity of the paper she used. Maybe he was too caught up in his unexplained feelings for the young woman. He might have been thinking with his heart instead of his head when he'd agreed to try to sell some of her artwork. Now he was going to have to face Kelly when she stopped by the store again and tell her nothing had sold.

That's not entirely true, he reminded himself. *I took one of her pictures to give Betsy Nelson, and I plan to pay Kelly her share for it. Maybe I should buy a second picture, then frame it and hang it in my house.* Mike smiled, feeling a sense of satisfaction because of his idea. Kelly wouldn't have to know who'd bought the drawings. She'd probably be happy just getting the money.

With that decided, Mike removed the picture of Kelly's two mules and stuck it under the front counter. He would take it home when he was done for the day.

Mike pulled out an envelope and wrote Kelly's name on it. Then he withdrew some money from the cash box and tucked it inside. Hopefully he'd be able to sell her other drawing before Kelly came by the store again.

"I need to get busy and quit thinking about Kelly McGregor," Mike muttered as he grabbed a broom and started sweeping the floor. Thoughts of the young woman with dark brown eyes and long, coffee-colored hair were consuming too much of his time.

Mike had just put the broom away in the storage closet when the front door opened. He pivoted, and his heartbeat quickened. Kelly McGregor stood there, her straw hat askew, and her long gray skirt, wrinkled, dirty, and damp. She looked a mess, yet he thought she was beautiful.

Mike swallowed hard and moved toward her. "Kelly. It's good to see you again."

"Hello, Mike Cooper," Kelly said, feeling timid and unsure of herself.

He smiled, and the dimple in his chin seemed to be winking at her.

She took a tentative step forward. "Mama's sick and needs some cough syrup. Have ya got any on hand?"

"I think there's still several bottles on the back shelf." Mike pointed to the other end of the store. "Would you like me to get one for you?"

She nodded. "If ya don't mind."

"Not at all." Mike headed in the direction he'd pointed, and Kelly turned her attention to the wall nearest the door. One of her drawings of children playing along the canal was there, but the other two were nowhere in sight. A feeling of excitement coursed through her veins. Had Mike sold them? Did she have some money coming now? Dare she ask?

When Mike returned a few minutes later, she was still studying her drawing. She glanced over at him. He held a bottle of cough syrup and stood so close she could smell the aroma of soap, which indicated that he at least was wearing clean clothes. Mike's hair was nicely combed, too. She, on the other hand, looked terrible. He probably thought she was a filthy pig. Should she explain about falling into the canal? Would he even care?

"You're quite talented," Mike said, bringing Kelly's thoughts to a halt. "Have you done any more pictures lately?"

"I did have three more ready, but Mama's been sick, so Papa and me have had to share all the chores." She glanced down at her soiled skirt and frowned. "As you can see, I fell in the canal earlier today, trying to jump from the boat back to the towpath. My drawings were in my pocket, and they got ruined."

Mike shook his head slowly. "Sorry to hear that. I did wonder why your skirt was so rumpled and wet." He moved toward the counter, and Kelly followed. "Sorry you're having to do double duty, but maybe this will make you feel better." He set the cough syrup down, pulled open a drawer beneath the counter, withdrew an envelope, and handed it to Kelly.

She took the envelope and studied it a few seconds. Her name was written on the front. "What's this?"

"It's your share of the money for two of the drawings you left with me."

She smiled up at him. "You really sold two of my pictures?"

Mike's ears turned slightly red, and he looked a little flustered. Was he embarrassed because he hadn't sold all three?

"I. . .uh. . .found someone who really appreciates your talent," he said, staring down at the wooden counter.

Kelly's smile widened. "I'm so glad. Once Mama gets better, I'll have a bit more time to draw, and maybe when we stop by here again I'll have a few more pictures to give you."

Mike's smile seemed to be forced, and his face had turned red like his ears. Something seemed to be troubling him, and Kelly aimed to find out what it was.

"Is everything all right? You look kinda upset."

Mike lifted his gaze. "Everything's fine. Feel free to bring me as many drawings as you like."

Kelly felt a sense of relief wash over her. If she could get Mama back on her feet, she'd have more time to draw. Mike wanted her to bring more pictures, she'd already sold two, and things were looking hopeful. She slipped the envelope into her apron pocket and turned toward the door.

"Aren't you forgetting something?" Mike called after her.

Kelly whirled around and felt the heat of a blush spread over her face when Mike held up the bottle of cough syrup. She giggled self-consciously and fished in her pocket for the coins to pay for her purchase.

Mike's fingers brushed hers as she dropped the money into his hand, and Kelly felt an unexpected shiver tickle her spine. What was there about Mike Cooper that made her feel so giddy and out of breath? Was it the crooked smile beneath his perfectly shaped mustache? Those hazel eyes that seemed capable of looking into her soul? The lock of sandy brown hair that fell across his forehead?

Kelly snatched up the bottle of cough syrup, mumbled a quick thanks, and fled.

Mike couldn't believe the way Kelly had run out of the store. Had he said or done something to upset her? He'd thought they were getting along pretty well, and Kelly had seemed pleased about her drawings being sold.

Maybe she suspects I'm the one who bought the pictures. But how could she know that? He'd been careful not to give her too much information, so she couldn't have guessed he was the one. He hadn't actually lied to her, but he didn't see the need to tell Kelly he was the one either. She might have taken it the wrong way.

Seeing Kelly again had only reinforced the strong feelings Mike was having for her. When their hands touched briefly during the money exchange, he had felt as though he'd been struck by a bolt of lightning. Had Kelly felt it, too? Could that have been the reason for her sudden departure? Or maybe she just needed to get back to work. The canal boaters always seemed to be in a hurry to get to and from their pickup and delivery points. That was probably all it was. Kelly's dad had no doubt told her to hurry, and she was only complying with his wishes.

How am I going to get to know Kelly better if she stops by the store only once in a while, then stays just long enough to buy something and hurries off again? Mike closed his eyes. *Lord, would You please work it out so Kelly and I can spend more time together?*

Mike was still standing behind the counter, mulling things over, when Amos McGregor entered the store.

"Mr. McGregor, your daughter was just here buying some cough syrup for your wife."

"Don'tcha think I know that?" the boatman snapped. His bright red hair stuck out at odd angles, like he hadn't combed it in a couple of days, and dark circles rimmed his eyes.

Mike shrugged. It was obvious the man wasn't in a good mood, and there was no point in saying anything that might rile him further.

"The wife's been sick for a couple of days," Amos mumbled. "That left me stuck doin' most of her chores." He stuffed his hands inside the pocket of his dark blue jacket and started for the back of the store.

"Can I help you find something?" Mike called after him.

"Need some of that newfangled soap that floats," came the muffled reply. "I told Kelly to get some, but as usual, she had her head in the clouds and forgot."

Mike skirted around the counter and went straight to the shelf where he kept the cleaning supplies and personal toiletries. "Here's what you're looking for, sir," he said, lifting a bar of soap for the man's inspection.

"Yep. That's it, all right." Amos shook his head slowly. "I dropped our last bar overboard by mistake and didn't wanna take the time to stop and fish it outa the canal." He grabbed another bar of soap and marched back to the counter. "Better to have a spare," he muttered.

Mike nodded and slipped the cakes of soap

into a paper sack. "Good idea." He handed the bag to Amos. "Need anything else?"

"Nope." Amos plunked some coins on the counter and started for the front door.

"Feel free to stop by anytime," Mike called after him. "And if you ever need a place to spend the night, I'll gladly let you stable your mules in my barn."

The boatman mumbled something under his breath and shut the door.

Mike shook his head. "I wonder why that man's such a grouch? No wonder Kelly acts like a scared rabbit much of the time. Guess I'd better pray for the both of them."

CHAPTER 9

O n Saturday evening, much to Mike's surprise, Kelly and her mother stopped by the store.

"That cough syrup you sold Kelly a few days ago sure helped me sleep," Dorrie said as she stepped up beside Mike, who'd been stocking shelves near the front of the store.

Mike smiled. "I'm glad to hear that, Mrs. McGregor. Are you feeling better?"

She nodded. "I'm back to doin' most of

my own chores, too."

Mike glanced at Kelly out of the corner of his eye. She was standing by the candy counter, eyeing something she was obviously interested in. He started to move toward the young woman, but Dorrie's next words stopped him.

"Amos is feelin' poorly now, so we need more medicine." Her forehead wrinkled, and she blinked a couple of times. "Sure hope you've got some, 'cause I used up the bottle of cough syrup Kelly bought."

Mike nodded toward the back of the store. "There's a couple bottles on the second shelf to the right. Want me to get one for you?"

Dorrie glanced over at Kelly, still peering inside the candy counter, and she shook her head. "Why don'tcha see what kind of sweet treat my daughter would like, while I fetch the medicine?"

Mike didn't have to be asked twice. He set the tin of canned peaches he'd been holding down on the shelf and then hurried over to Kelly.

"How are you?" he asked. "Sure hope you're not getting sick, too."

"Nope. I'm healthy as a mule."

"Glad to hear it, but I'm sorry about your dad. Is he able to keep on working?"

"He made it through the day, even with his fits of coughing and fever. I think he's plannin' to tie up here and spend the night. We'll stay all day Sunday, so he can rest." Kelly's gaze went to her mother, who was at the back of the store. "Mama doesn't have all her strength back yet, either, so a good day's rest should do 'em both some good."

And you, Kelly, Mike thought as he studied her face. The dark circles under her eyes gave evidence to how tired she was.

"The last time your dad was in the store, I told him I'd be glad to stable your mules in my barn anytime he wanted to dock here for the night."

"That's right nice of you." Kelly gazed at the candy counter with a look of longing on her face.

Mike wondered how long it had been since she had eaten any candy. Without hesitation, he opened the hinged lid on the glass case. "Help yourself to whatever you like—my treat."

Kelly stiffened. "Oh no. I couldn't let you do that. Thanks to you sellin' a couple of my charcoal drawings, I've got money of my own now." She shrugged. "Although it's safely hidden in my room on the boat, and I'd have to go back and get it."

"Wouldn't you rather spend it on something more useful than candy?"

She pursed her lips. "Probably should be savin' my money, but I've sure got a hankerin' for some lemon drops."

Mike reached down and grabbed the glass jar filled with sugar-coated lemon drops. "Take as many as you like, and please consider it a present from me to you."

Kelly tipped her head to one side, as if contemplating his offer. Finally with a nervous giggle, she agreed.

He filled a small paper bag half full of candy

and handed it to her, hoping she wouldn't change her mind.

She took the sack and stuffed it in her apron pocket. "Thank you."

"You're welcome."

Kelly shuffled her feet, and her boots scraped noisily against the wooden planks. Why did she seem so nervous? Was it because her mother was nearby and might be listening in on their conversation?

Hoping to put her at ease, Mike reached out and touched Kelly's arm. She recoiled like she'd been bitten by a snake, and he quickly withdrew his hand.

"Sorry, I didn't mean to startle you."

Kelly shrugged. What was wrong? They'd had such a pleasant visit the last time she'd come by.

"Did you bring me any more drawings?" Mike asked, hoping the change of subject might ease the tension he felt filling up the space between them.

She shook her head. "I'm out of charcoal,

and for the last couple of days, Papa's been burnin' coal instead of wood in our cookstove. I haven't come across any cold campfires along the canal lately neither."

So that was the problem. Kelly was feeling bad because she hadn't been able to draw and she'd promised Mike she would have more pictures the next time she came by.

Mike had a brand-new set of sketching pencils for sale, along with some tubes of oil paints. He would have gladly given them to her but was sure she would say no. It had taken some persuasion to get her to take a few lemon drops, and they weren't worth half as much as the art supplies. Since Kelly did have some money of her own, she could probably purchase a box of pencils, but she might be saving up for something more important.

Suddenly, Mike had an idea. "I've got some burned charcoal chips in my home fireplace at the back of the store," he announced. "How 'bout I run in there and get them for you?"

Kelly hesitated a moment but finally

nodded. "That would be right nice."

Before she had a chance to change her mind, Mike hurried to the back of the store. He passed Kelly's mother on his way to the door leading to his attached house.

"I'll be right back, Mrs. McGregor. Take your time looking around for anything you might need."

Kelly watched Mike's retreating form as he disappeared behind the door at the back of his store. He seemed like such a caring young man. Probably would make someone a mighty fine husband. Maybe he and the preacher's daughter would link up. Betsy had seemed pretty friendly to him the last time Kelly saw the two of them together.

She frowned. Why did the idea of Mike and Betsy Nelson together make her feel so squeamish? She reached into the sack inside her pocket and withdrew a lemon drop, then popped the piece of candy into her mouth.

"We'll head on back to the boat as soon as the storekeeper returns and I pay for the cough syrup and a few other things I found," Mama said, driving Kelly's thoughts to the back of her mind.

Kelly slowly nodded her head.

"Mike Cooper seems like a nice young man," Mama remarked.

Kelly nodded again. "He offered to let us stable Herman and Hector in his barn for the night."

Mama's dark eyebrows lifted. "For free?"

"I think so. He never said a word about money."

"Hmm. . .guess as soon as we leave the store, you should get the mules fed and ready to bed down then."

"I'd be happy to," Kelly readily agreed. "I'm sure Hector and Herman will be right glad to have a bigger place to stay tonight than they have on board our boat."

"You're probably right." Mama smiled. "Say, I was thinkin'—since tomorrow's Sunday, and we won't be movin' on 'til early Monday morning, why don't the two of us head into town and go to church?"

Kelly opened her mouth to respond, but Mama rushed on. "It's been a good while since I've sat inside a real church and worshiped God with other Christian folks."

"Well, I. . .uh. . ." Kelly swallowed against the urge to say what was really on her mind. Being in church would make her feel uncomfortable—like others were looking down their noses at the poor boatman's daughter who wore men's boots and smelled like a dirty mule. Kelly had seen the way Betsy Nelson turned her nose up whenever the two of them met along the towpath. She wasn't good enough to sit inside a pretty church building; it was just that simple.

"I'm waitin' for your answer," Mama said, giving Kelly's shoulder a gentle tap.

"I was kinda hoping to get rested up tomorrow. Maybe do a bit of drawin'."

Mama's squinted eyes and furrowed brow

revealed her obvious concern. "You ain't feelin' poorly, too, I hope."

Kelly shook her head. "Just tired is all."

"And well you should be," Mama agreed. "The last few days, you and your dad have been workin' real hard trying to do all my chores plus keeping up with your own jobs as well." She gave Kelly a hug. "I think you're right. It might be good for us all to spend the day restin'."

Kelly felt bad about not being willing to attend church with her mother. She could tell by Mama's wistful expression that she really did miss Sunday services inside a church building. Reading the Bible every night after supper was a good thing, but it wasn't the same as being in fellowship with other believers.

She and her mother went to wait for Mike by the wooden sales counter.

A few seconds later, Mike entered the store, carrying a large paper sack. He handed it to Kelly and grinned. "This should get you by for a while."

She peered inside the bag. Several large clumps of charcoal, as well as some smaller ones, completely filled it. Mike was right. These would last a good while, and tonight she planned to start putting them to use. "Thanks," she murmured.

He winked at her. "You're more than welcome."

Kelly cleared her throat, feeling kind of warm and jittery inside. Maybe she was coming down with whatever had been ailing her folks. A day of rest might do her more good than she realized.

CHAPTER 10

———— ❋ ————

Sunday morning dawned with a blue, cloudless sky. It would be the perfect day for Kelly to enjoy the warm sun and draw. She hurried through her breakfast and morning chores, anxious for some time alone. Mama would be tending to Papa's needs for the next little while, and after that, she would probably take a rest herself.

Papa had taken to his bed last night and not even shown his face at the breakfast table.

Kelly figured he must be pretty sick if he wasn't interested in food, for her dad usually had a ravenous appetite. She had taken him a tray with a cup of tea and bowl of oatmeal a little while ago, but Papa turned his nose up at both and said he wanted to be left alone—needed some sleep, that was all.

It seemed strange for Kelly to see her dad, who was usually up early and raring to go, curled up in a fetal position with a patch-work quilt pulled up to his ears. His breathing sounded labored, and he wheezed and coughed like the steam train that ran beside the canal, despite the medicine Mama had been spoon-feeding him since their visit to Mike's store last evening.

Thinking about Mike Cooper made Kelly remember their mules had been sleeping in his barn all night. She needed to feed and groom the animals, then take them outdoors for some fresh air and exercise. Wouldn't do for the mules to get lazy because they'd stopped for a bit. As soon as she was finished tending the critters, Kelly hoped to finally have some free time.

As she headed for the barn, which sat directly behind Mike's house, Kelly hummed her favorite song—"Hunks-a-go Pudding." Would Mama feel up to fixing a big meal today? Would it include a roast with some yummy hunks-a-go pudding? Kelly sure hoped so. It had been a good long while since she'd enjoyed the succulent taste of roast beef and hunks-a-go pudding, where the batter was put in the fat left over from the meat and then fried in a pan on top of the stove.

Forcing thoughts of food to the back of her mind, Kelly opened the barn door and peered inside. Except for the gentle braying of the mules, all was quiet. The sweet smell of hay wafted up to her nose, and she sniffed deeply. She stepped inside and was almost to the stall where Hector and Herman were stabled when she heard another sound. Someone was singing.

"Sweet hour of prayer, sweet hour of prayer,

that calls me from a world of care."

Kelly plodded across the dirt floor, and the sound of the clear, masculine voice grew closer. She recognized it as belonging to Mike Cooper.

"And bids me at my Father's throne, make all my wants and wishes known."

Kelly halted, feeling like an intruder on Mike's quiet time alone with God. He must be deeply religious, for not only was he kindhearted, but he sang praises to God. Whenever Kelly sang, it was some silly canaler's song like "Hunks-a-go Pudding" or "You Rusty Canaler, You'll Never Get Rich." As a young child she would often sing "Jesus Loves Me," but she'd been a lot happier back then. Sarah had still been living with them, helping share the burden of walking the mules and visiting with Kelly for hours on end. Papa expected twice as much from Kelly now that Sarah was gone. But was that any excuse to quit worshiping the Lord?

Kelly knew the answer deep in her soul.

She was angry with God for not changing Papa's heart. She was angry with Papa for being so stubborn and hot-tempered. And she was angry with Sarah for running off and leaving her to face Papa's temper and do all the work.

I'll show them. I'll show everyone that Kelly McGregor doesn't need anyone to get along in this world. I'm gonna make it on my own someday.

When Mike's song ended, Kelly moved forward again. She could see him sitting on a small wooden stool, milking a fat brown and white cow.

She cleared her throat real loud to make her presence known and stepped into the stall where Herman and Hector had bedded down for the night.

"Good morning," Mike called to her.

"Mornin'," she responded.

"Looks like it's gonna be a beautiful day."

"Yep. Right nice."

"What plans have you made for this Lord's Day?" he asked.

Kelly patted Herman's flank and leaned into the sturdy mule. "As soon as I get these two ready, I plan to take 'em outside for some exercise and fresh air."

Mike didn't say anything in reply, and Kelly could hear the steady *plunk, plink, plunk*, as the cow's milk dropped into the bucket. It was a soothing sound, and she found herself wishing she had a real, honest-to-goodness home with a barn, chicken coop, and maybe a bit of land. Nine months out of the year, her home was the inside of a canal boat, and during the winter, it was a cramped, dingy flat at a boardinghouse in Easton. Papa seemed to like their vagabond life, but Kelly hated it—more and more the older she got. Someday she hoped to leave it all behind. Oh, for the chance to fulfill her dreams.

Mike grabbed the bucket of milk and headed for the stall where Kelly's mules had been stabled. He was finally being given the chance to spend a few minutes alone with Kelly, and he aimed to take full advantage. If things went as he hoped, he would have the pleasure of her company for several hours today.

Mike leaned against the wooden beam outside the mules' stall and watched Kelly as she fed and groomed her beasts of burden. She wasn't wearing her usual straw hat this morning, and her lustrous brown hair hung down her back in long, loose waves. His fingers itched to reach out and touch those silky tresses.

"You're good with the mules," he murmured.

Kelly jumped, apparently startled and unaware that he'd been watching her. "Hector and Herman are easy to work with."

Mike drew in a deep breath. *May as well get this over with.* "I...uh...was wondering if you'd like to go on a picnic with me later today."

Kelly turned her head to look directly at him, and she blinked a couple of times. "A picnic? You and me?"

He nodded, then chuckled. "That's what I had in mind."

"Well, I was plannin' to spend some time drawin', and—"

"No reason you can't draw after we share our picnic lunch."

She hesitated a few seconds. "Mama may need my help with somethin', and my folks might not approve of me goin' on a picnic."

Mike smiled. At least she hadn't said no. He took that as a good sign. "While you finish up with the mules, how about I go talk to your parents?"

Kelly's forehead wrinkled. "I don't know if that's such a good idea."

"If they say it's all right, would you be willing to eat a picnic lunch with me?"

She nodded. Mike grinned. "Great! I'll take this milk into the house, get cleaned up a bit, and run down to the boat to speak with your folks."

"Papa's still in bed," Kelly said. "He ain't feelin' much better today than he was last night."

"Sorry to hear it. I'll ask your mother."

Mike hurried out of the barn, and he hummed "Sweet Hour of Prayer" all the way. God was already answering his prayer for the day, and he felt like he was ten feet tall.

Kelly couldn't believe her mother had actually given permission for Mike Cooper to take her on a picnic. Maybe she felt bad because Kelly worked so hard and rarely got a day off. Or it might be that Mama needed some quiet time herself today, so she thought it would be good if Kelly were gone awhile.

The idea of a picnic did seem kind of nice. It would be a chance for Kelly to relax and enjoy Mike's company, as well as the good food he'd promised to prepare. On the other hand, spending time alone with the fine-looking storekeeper might not be such a good thing. What if he got the notion she was interested in him? Would Mike expect her to do more things with him when she was in the area? In some ways, she hoped they could. Life along the canal was lonely, especially when her only companions were a pair of mules.

Kelly stood in her tiny room and studied her reflection in the mirror that she kept in the trunk at the foot of her bed. Did she look presentable enough to accompany Mike Cooper on a picnic? Mike always smelled so clean, and he wore crisp trousers and shirts without holes or wrinkles. It was hard to believe he had no mother or wife caring for his needs. He must be very capable, she decided.

Mike had said he would meet Kelly in front of his store a little before noon. This gave her plenty of time to get ready, and she'd even taken a bath in the galvanized tub and washed her hair, using that new floating soap Mama liked so well.

Kelly grabbed a lock of hair, swung it over her shoulder, and sniffed deeply. "Smells clean enough to me." She glanced down at her dark green skirt and long-sleeved white blouse with puffy sleeves. Both were plain and unfashionable, but Kelly didn't care a hoot about fashion, only comfort and looking presentable enough to be seen in public. Her clothes were clean; Mama had washed them yesterday. At least today she wasn't likely to offend Mike by smelling like one of her mules.

Kelly took out her drawing tablet and a piece of charcoal and stuffed them in her oversized skirt pocket. Then she grabbed her straw hat and one of Mama's old quilts. At least they would have something soft to sit on during their picnic lunch. She left the room and tiptoed quietly past her parents' bedroom. It wouldn't be good to wake Papa. He'd probably be furious if he knew she was taking the day off to go on a picnic—especially with a man. He might think she was going to up and run off the way Sarah had. Well, that would never happen!

As Kelly stepped off the boat, she caught a glimpse of Reverend Nelson and his daughter, Betsy. They were standing in front of Mike's store, and several boatmen and their families had gathered around.

It made no sense to Kelly. Shouldn't the preacher have been at his church, pounding the wooden pulpit and shouting at the congregation to repent and turn from their wicked ways? Instead, he was leading the group of people in song, and his daughter was playing along with her zither.

Kelly hoped to avoid the throng entirely, but Mike, who stood on the fringes, motioned her to join him. He was holding a wicker basket, and Kelly figured he was probably ready to head out on their picnic. If she hung back until the church service was over, they would lose some of their time together.

Mike crooked his finger at Kelly again, and she inched her way forward. *Guess I may as well see what he's plannin' to do.*

Chapter 11

---·❖·---

Mike smiled at Kelly when she stepped up beside him.

"What's goin' on?" she whispered.

"Reverend Nelson finished his worship service early today, so he and Betsy decided to bring a bit of revival to the boatmen and their families who stayed in the area for the night."

"Do you attend their church in town?" Kelly asked.

Mike shrugged his shoulders. "Sometimes." The truth was, he used to go every Sunday, but here of late he'd been feeling mighty uncomfortable around Betsy Nelson. He'd stayed home the last couple weeks, praying and reading his Bible in solitude. He knew he shouldn't be using Betsy's overbearing, flirtatious ways as an excuse to stay away from church, but it was getting harder to deal with her. Especially since Kelly McGregor had come into his life.

He stared down at Kelly, small and delicate, yet strong and reliable. Where did she stand as far as spiritual things were concerned? He needed to find out soon, before he lost his heart to the beautiful young woman.

"Ready to head out on our picnic?" Kelly questioned.

Now was as good a time as any to see how interested she was in church.

"I thought maybe we'd stick around until Reverend Nelson is done preaching," Mike said. "It's been awhile since I've heard a good sermon." He studied Kelly's face to gauge her reaction. She looked a bit hesitant, but agreeably she nodded. He breathed a sigh of relief.

"Should we take a seat on the grass?" he asked, motioning to a spot a few feet away.

She followed him there and spread out the quilt she'd been holding so tightly.

Mike set the picnic basket down, and they both took a seat on the blanket. Leaning back on his elbows, Mike joined the group singing "Amazing Grace." His spirits soared as the music washed over him like gentle waves lapping against the shore. He loved to sing praises to God, and when the mood hit, he enjoyed blowing on the old mouth harp that had belonged to Grandpa Cooper.

He glanced over at Kelly. She wasn't singing, but her eyes were closed, and her face was lifted toward the sun. *She must be praying. That's a good indication that she knows the Lord personally.*

He smiled to himself. The day had started out even better than he'd expected.

Kelly opened her eyes and looked around. About two dozen people were seated on the ground. Some were singing, some lifted their hands in praise, and others quietly listened. She couldn't believe she'd let Mike talk her into staying around for this outdoor church service. It was a beautiful spring day, and she wanted to be away from the crowd, where she could listen to the sounds of nature and draw to her heart's content. When she'd agreed to accompany Mike on a picnic, the plan hadn't included church.

Kelly knew her attitude was wrong. She'd asked Jesus to forgive her sins several years ago. She should take pleasure in worshiping God. Besides, out here among the other boatmen and their families, Kelly didn't stick out like a sore thumb. Nobody but the preacher and his daughter were dressed in fine clothes, so Kelly blended right in with her unfashionable long cotton skirt and plain white blouse.

The singing was over, and the reverend had begun to preach. Kelly's gaze wandered until she noticed a young boy who sat several feet away. He had bright red hair, and his face and arms were covered with freckles. The child's looks weren't what captured Kelly's attention, though. It was the small green toad he was holding in his grubby hands. He stroked the critter's head as though it were a pet.

He's probably poor and doesn't own many toys. If his papa's a boatman, they travel up and down the canal most of the year, so the little guy can't have any real pets.

Kelly knew that wasn't entirely true. Many canalers owned dogs that either walked along the towpath or rode in the boat. She figured the little red-haired boy's dad was probably too cranky or too stingy to let his son own a dog or a cat. *Kind of like my dad. He'd never allow me to have a pet.*

Kelly's thoughts were halted as Preacher Nelson shouted, "God wants you to turn from your sins and repent!"

She sat up a little straighter and tried to look attentive when she noticed Mike look over at her. Had he caught her daydreaming?

Did he think she was a sinner who needed to repent?

After the pastor's final prayer, he announced, "My daughter, Betsy, will now close our service with a solo."

Betsy stood up and began to strum her zither as she belted out the first verse of "Sweet By and By." As the young woman came to the last note, her voice cracked, and her face turned redder than a radish.

Kelly stifled a chuckle behind her hand. *Serves the snooty woman right for thinkin' she's better'n me.*

"He that is without sin among you, let him first cast a stone at her." Kelly gulped as she remembered that verse of scripture from the book of John. Mama had quoted it many times over the years.

The preacher's daughter might be uppity and kind of pushy at times, but Kelly knew she was no better in God's eyes. Fact of the matter, Kelly felt that she was probably worse, for she often harbored resentment in her heart toward Papa. She resolved to try to do better.

When the service was over, Mike stood and grabbed their picnic basket. Kelly gathered up her quilt and tucked it under one arm. She'd thought they would head right off for their picnic, but Mike moved toward Preacher Nelson. Not knowing what else to do, Kelly followed.

"That was a fine sermon you preached," Mike said, shaking Reverend Nelson's hand.

The older man beamed. "Thank you, Mike. I'm glad you enjoyed it."

Betsy, who stood next to her father, smiled at Mike and fluttered her eyelashes. "How about the singing? Did you enjoy that, too?"

Mike nodded. It was downright sickening the way Betsy kept eyeing him, as though she wanted to kiss the man, of all things.

Kelly nudged Mike in the ribs with her elbow. "Are we goin' on that picnic or not?"

"Yes. . .yes, of course," he stammered.

Why was Mike acting so nervous all of a sudden? Did being around Betsy Nelson do this to him? Kelly opened her mouth to say something, but Betsy cut her right off.

"You're going on a picnic, Mike?" Her eyelids fluttered again. "It's such a beautiful day, and I haven't been on a picnic since early last fall. Would you mind if I tag along?"

"Well, uh. . ." Mike turned to Kelly, as though he expected her to say something.

When she made no response, Betsy said, "You wouldn't mind if I joined you and Mike, would you, Kelly?"

Kelly's irritation flared up like fireflies buzzing on a muggy summer day. She didn't want to make an issue, so she merely shrugged her shoulders and made circles in the dirt with the toe of her boot.

"Great! It's all settled then." Betsy grinned like an eager child. "Have you got enough food for three, Mike?"

"Sure, I made plenty of fried chicken and biscuits."

Betsy turned to her father then. "I won't be gone long, Papa."

He smiled. "You go on with the young people and have yourself a good time. I want to visit with several folks, and if I'm fortunate enough to be invited to join one of the families for a meal, I probably won't be home until evening."

"Everything is perfect then. I'll see you at home later on." Betsy handed her father the zither and slipped her hand through the crook of Mike's arm. "So, where should we have this picnic?"

"Guess we'll look for a nice spot up the canal a bit." When Mike looked at Kelly, she noticed his face was a deep shade of red. Was he wondering why he'd invited her on a picnic? Did he wish he could spend time alone with Betsy Nelson? Should Kelly make up some excuse as to why she couldn't go? Maybe it would be best if she went off by herself for the day.

Mike pulled away from Betsy and grabbed hold of Kelly's hand. "Let's be off," he announced. "I'm hungry as a bear!"

CHAPTER 12

———— ❋ ————

Kelly, Mike, and Betsy sat in silence on the quilt. The picnic basket was empty, and everyone admitted to being full. There had been plenty of food to go around.

Kelly leaned back on her elbows, soaking up the sun's warming rays and listening to the canal waters lapping against the bank. She felt relaxed and content and had almost forgotten her irritation over the preacher's daughter joining their picnic.

Seeing a couple of ducks on the water

reminded Kelly that she'd brought along her drawing tablet and a piece of charcoal. She sat up and withdrew both from her skirt pocket, then quickly began to sketch. A flash of green on the mallard's head made her once again wish she could work with colored paints. Folks might be apt to buy a picture with color, as it looked more like the real thing.

"In another month or so the canal will be filled with swimmers," Betsy said, her high-pitched voice cutting into the serenely quiet moment.

"You're right about that," Mike agreed. "It scares me the way some youngsters swim so close to the canal boats. It's a wonder one of them doesn't get killed."

"I hear there's plenty of accidents on the canal," Betsy put in.

"Kelly could probably tell us a lot of stories in that regard," Mike said.

Kelly's mind took her back to a couple years ago, when she'd witnessed one of the lock tender's children fall between a boat and the lock. The little boy had been killed instantly— crushed to death. It was a pitiful sight to see the child's mother weeping and wailing.

Kelly had seen a few small children fall overboard and drown. Most folks who had little ones kept them tied to a rope so that wouldn't happen, but some who'd been careless paid the price with the loss of a child.

"Yep," Kelly murmured, "there's been quite a few deaths on the Lehigh Navigation System."

Mike groaned. "I was afraid of the water when I was a boy, so I never learned to swim as well as I probably should have. So I don't often go in the canal except to wade or do a couple of dives off the locks now and then."

"If you can't swim too good, aren't you afraid to dive?" Kelly asked.

He shrugged his shoulders. "I can manage to kick my way to the surface of the water, then paddle like a dog back to the lock."

"Hmm. . .I see."

"What about you?" Betsy asked, looking directly at Kelly. "As dirty as you get trudging up and down the dusty towpath, I imagine you must jump into the canal quite frequently in order to get cleaned off."

Kelly sniffed deeply, feeling a sudden need to defend herself. "I learned to swim when I was a little girl, so I have no fear of drowning." *Just scared to death of water snakes*, her inner voice reminded. She saw no need to reveal her reservations about swimming in the canal. No use giving the preacher's daughter one more thing to look down her nose about.

Mike shifted on the quilt and leaned closer to Kelly. She could feel his warm breath against her neck and found it to be a distraction.

"That's a nice picture you're making," Mike whispered. "Is the charcoal I gave you working out okay?"

"It's fine," she answered as she kept on drawing.

"Maybe you can get a few pictures done today so I can take them back to the store and try to sell them."

She nodded. "Maybe so."

"How about you and me going for a walk, Mike?" Betsy asked, cutting into their conversation.

Mike moved away from Kelly, and she felt a keen sense of disappointment, which made no sense, since she wasn't the least bit interested in the storekeeper. She'd already decided Betsy Nelson would make a better match for Mike than someone like herself.

"Kelly, would you like to walk with me and Betsy?" Mike asked.

She shook her head. "I'd rather stay here with my tablet and charcoal. You two go ahead. I'll be fine."

Betsy stood up and held her hand out to Mike. "I'm ready if you are."

He made a grunting sound as he clambered to his feet. "We'll be back soon, Kelly."

Keeping her focus on the ducks swimming directly in front of her, Kelly mumbled, "Sure, okay."

———— ❋ ————

Mike wasn't the least bit happy about leaving Kelly alone while he and Betsy went for a walk. This was supposed to be his and Kelly's picnic— a chance for them to get better acquainted. It should have been Kelly he was walking with, not the preacher's daughter.

Betsy clung to his arm like they were a courting couple, and she chattered a mile a minute. If only he could figure out some way to discourage her without being rude. Mike didn't want to hurt Betsy's feelings, but he didn't want to lead her on, either.

"Maybe we should head back," he said, when Betsy stopped talking long enough for him to get in a word.

She squeezed his arm a little tighter and kept on walking. "Why would you want to head back? It's a beautiful day, and the fresh air and exercise will do us both some good."

Mike opened his mouth to reply, but she cut him right off.

"I missed seeing you in church this morning."

He cleared his throat a few times, feeling like a little boy who was about to be reprimanded for being naughty. "Well, I—"

"Papa says we need young men like yourself as active members in the church," Betsy said, chopping him off again.

Mike shrugged as a feeling of guilt slid over him. He knew what the Bible said about men being the spiritual leaders. He also was aware that he needed to take a more active part in evangelizing the world. Maybe he would speak to Reverend Nelson about holding regular church services along the canal. Mike could donate some of his Bibles for people who didn't have one of their own. As far as attending the Nelsons' church, Mike wasn't sure that was such a good idea. It would mean spending more time with Betsy. It wasn't that he disliked the woman, but her chattering and pushiness got on his nerves.

"Mike, are you listening to me?"

He pushed his thoughts aside and focused on the woman who was tugging on his shirtsleeve. "What were you saying?"

"I was talking about mission work," Betsy replied in an exasperated tone. "I said we have a mission opportunity right here along the canal."

He nodded. "I agree. I was just thinking that if your father wanted to hold regular Sunday services out in front of my store, I'd be happy to furnish folks with Bibles."

Betsy's thin lips curled into a smile. "That sounds like a wonderful idea. I'll speak to Papa about it this evening."

Mike was amazed at Betsy's exuberance. She either shared his desire to tell others about Jesus or was merely looking forward to spending more time with him.

He grimaced. *I shouldn't be thinking the worst.* Mike knew he was going to have to work on his attitude, especially where the preacher's daughter was concerned. She did have some good points, but she wasn't the kind of woman Mike was looking for.

A vision of Kelly flashed into his mind. Dark eyes that bore right through him; long dark hair cascading down her back; a smile that could light up any room. But it was more than Kelly's good looks and winning smile that had captured Mike's attention. There was a tenderness and vulnerability about Kelly McGregor that drew Mike to her like a thirsty horse heads for water. Sometimes, she seemed like an innocent child needing to be rescued from something that was causing her pain. The next minute, Kelly appeared confident and self-assured. She was like a jigsaw puzzle, and he wanted to put all the complicated pieces of her together.

"Mike, you're not listening to me again."

He turned his head in Betsy's direction. "What were you saying?"

"I was wondering if you would like to come over for supper one night next week."

He groped for words that wouldn't be a lie. "I. . .uh. . .am expecting a shipment of goods soon, and I need to clean off some shelves and get the place organized before the load arrives."

Betsy's lower lip jutted out. "Surely you won't be working every evening."

Mike nodded. "I could be."

Her eyebrows drew together, nearly meeting at the middle. "I was hoping to tempt you with my chicken and dumplings. Papa says they're the best he's ever tasted."

"I'm sure they are." Mike gave Betsy's arm a gentle pat. "Maybe some other time."

"I hope so," she replied.

Should I be frank and tell her I'm not interested in pursuing a personal relationship? Mike stopped walking and swung around, taking Betsy with him, since she still held on to his arm. "We'd better head back now."

"Why so soon?"

"We left Kelly alone, and I don't feel right about that."

"I'm sure she's fine. She's not a little girl, you know."

Mike knew all right. Every time Kelly smiled at him or tipped her head to one side as she spoke his name, he was fully aware that she was a desirable young woman, not the child who used to drop by his store with her parents. He was anxious to get back to their picnic spot and see what Kelly had drawn.

"Mike, please slow down. I can barely keep up with you," Betsy panted when Mike started walking again.

"Sorry, but I invited Kelly to join me for a picnic today, and she probably thinks I've abandoned her."

Betsy moaned. "I didn't realize you two were courting. Why didn't you say so? If I'd known, I certainly would not have intruded on your time together."

Mike's ears were burning, and he knew they had turned bright red, the way they always did whenever he felt nervous or got flustered about something.

"Kelly and I are not officially courting," he mumbled. *Though I sure wish we were.*

Betsy opened her mouth as if to say something, but he spoke first.

"Even though we're not courting, I did invite her on a picnic. So, it's only right that I spend some time with her, don't you think?"

Betsy let out a deep sigh, but she nodded. "Far be it from me to keep you from your Christian duty."

"Thanks for understanding." Mike hurried up the towpath, with Betsy still clutching his arm. Soon Kelly came into view, and Mike halted his footsteps at the sight before him. Stretched out on the quilt, her dark hair fanned out like a pillow, Kelly had fallen asleep. The sketching tablet was in one hand, and a chunk of charcoal was in the other. She looked like an angel. Would she be his angel someday?

CHAPTER 13

The following day, Mike was surprised when Kelly's dad entered his store shortly after he'd opened for business.

"Mr. McGregor, how are you feeling this morning?" Mike asked.

"I'll live," came the curt reply.

"I hope the days you spent docked here gave you ample time to rest up and get that cough under control."

Amos coughed and grunted in response.

Wanda E. Brunstetter

"As I said, I'll live, but it looks like we'll be stuck here another day or so, 'cause thanks to you, one of my mules came up lame this mornin'."

Mike frowned. "Really? They both seemed fine yesterday."

"Herman's not fine now. He went and got his leg cut up on a bale of wire you carelessly left layin' around." Kelly's dad leveled Mike with a challenging look.

Feeling a headache coming on, Mike massaged his forehead with his fingertips. "Weren't your mules in their stalls last night?"

"Yeah, in your barn."

"Then I don't understand how one of them could have gotten cut with the wire, which was nowhere near the stalls."

"Guess the door wasn't latched tight and they got out. At least Herman did, for he's the one with the cut leg."

Mike opened his mouth to respond, but Amos rushed on. "You got any liniment for me to put on the poor critter?"

"I'm sure I do." Mike hurried to the area of the store where he kept all the medicinal supplies, and Amos stayed right on his heels. The man seemed grumpier than usual today. Was it because he was so upset about the mule's injury and blamed Mike for the mishap?

Mike had no more than taken the medicine off the shelf, when Amos snatched it out of his hands. The older man stomped up to the counter and demanded, "How much do I owe ya for this?"

"I normally charge a quarter for that liniment, but since you feel the accident was my fault, there'll be no charge," Mike answered as he moved to the other side of the counter. He knew the McGregors weren't financially well off, and now that they couldn't travel because of a lame mule, they would be set back even further.

Amos slapped a quarter down. "I won't be beholdin' to no man, so I'll pay ya what the stuff is worth." He grimaced. "I'm losin' money with each passing day. First I got slowed

153

down when Dorrie was sick and I was tryin' to cook, clean, and steer the boat. Then I came down with the bug and was laid up for a couple of days. Now I've got me a lame mule, and it should never have happened!"

"I'm sorry for your inconvenience, Mr. McGregor," Mike said apologetically.

"Yeah, well, at the rate things are goin', it'll be the end of the week before I can get back up to Mauch Chunk for another load of coal."

"Could you go on ahead with just one mule? I'd be happy to stable Herman until you come back this way."

Amos scowled at Mike. "Hector might be strong enough to pull the boat when it's empty, but not with a load of coal. Don'tcha know anything, boy?"

Mike clenched his teeth. Even though he didn't know everything about canal boating, he wasn't stupid. Should he defend himself to Kelly's dad or ignore the discourteous remark? Mike opted for the second choice. "I hope your mule's leg heals quickly, Mr. McGregor, and I'm sorry about the wire. If you need anything else, please don't hesitate to ask."

Amos coughed, blew his nose on the hanky he'd withdrawn from the pocket of his overalls, and sauntered out the door, slamming it behind him.

Mike sank to the wooden stool behind the counter and shook his head. At least one good thing would come from the McGregors being waylaid another day or two. It would give him a chance to see Kelly again. Yesterday's picnic had been a big disappointment to Mike. First, Betsy had invited herself to join them, and then, she'd hung on to him most of the day. Kelly had fallen asleep while she was waiting for him and Betsy to return from their walk. He'd wakened her when they got back to the picnic site, but Kelly seemed distant after that and said she needed to head for the boat. Mike offered to walk with her, but she handed him her finished picture of two ducks on the water and said she could find her own way. She'd even insisted that

Mike see the preacher's daughter safely home.

Mike reached up to scratch the back of his head. He had to let Kelly know he wasn't interested in Betsy. He cared about Kelly, and he wanted her to realize that. He just had to figure out how to go about revealing his true feelings without scaring her off.

Kelly couldn't believe they were stranded in front of Mike's store yet another day, possibly more. And as she followed Papa's curt instructions to get off the boat and put some medicine on Herman's leg, she shook her head over Papa's refusal to let the mules be stabled in Mike's barn any longer. It wasn't Mike's fault Herman had broken free from his stall and cut his leg on a roll of wire that had been sitting near the barn door. Now Herman and Hector were both tied to a maple tree growing several feet off the towpath, not far from where their boat was docked. Tonight, they would be bedded down in the compartment set aside for them in the bow of the boat.

Kelly squatted beside Herman's right front leg and slathered on some of the medicine. "I don't see why I have to do this," she muttered. "I'd planned to get some drawin' done today, but Papa will probably find more chores for me to do when I return to the boat."

A sense of guilt for her selfish thoughts washed over Kelly. She knew her dad still wasn't feeling well, and he had a right to get some rest while they were laid over. Trouble was, she wanted to draw. At the rate she was going, she would never have anything to give Mike to try to sell in his store. She had given him the picture of the ducks she'd drawn during yesterday's picnic, but that was all.

Thinking about the picnic caused an ache in Kelly's soul. She didn't understand why Mike had invited her, then asked Betsy Nelson to join them.

Well, not asked, exactly, she reminded herself. If Kelly's memory served her right, it was Betsy who had done the asking. Mike only agreed she could accompany them on the picnic. Might could be that he had no real interest in Betsy at all.

" 'Course I don't care if he does," she murmured.

Herman brayed, and Hector followed suit, as if in answer to her complaints.

When Kelly stood up, Herman nuzzled her arm with his nose. She chuckled and patted his neck. "You should be good as new in a day or so, Herman the Determined. Then we can be on our way again."

On impulse, Kelly reached into her apron pocket and withdrew the drawing pad and piece of charcoal she often carried with her. She flopped onto the ground and began to sketch the two mules as they grazed on the green grass.

Some time later, she stood up. She had two pictures of Herman and Hector to take over to Mike's.

When she entered the store, Kelly was pleased to see that Mike had no customers, and he seemed genuinely glad to see her.

"I was sorry to hear about Herman's leg," he said, moving toward Kelly. "Your dad thinks it's my fault because there was a roll of wire by the barn door."

She pursed her lips. "Papa always looks for someone to blame. Don't fret about it, 'cause it sure wasn't your doin'. If anyone's to blame, it's Papa. He's the one who fed and watered the mules last night, so he probably didn't see that the door to their stall was shut tight." She frowned. "Of course, he'd never admit it."

Mike grinned at Kelly, and her stomach did a little flip-flop. She licked her lips and took a step forward. "I. . .uh. . .brought you a couple more drawings."

She held the pictures out to Mike, and he took them. "Thanks, these are nice. I'll get them put on display right away."

"Sure wish they had a little color to 'em. Herman and Hector are brown, not black, but my picture don't show it."

"Maybe you could buy a set of watercolors

or oil paints," Mike suggested.

She shook her head. "Don't have enough money for that yet." Kelly knew she needed to save all her money if she was ever going to earn enough to be on her own or open an art gallery.

"Have you considered making your own watercolors?"

Her forehead wrinkled. "How could I do that?"

"I noticed some coffee stains on my tablecloth this morning," Mike said. "Funny thing was, they were all a different shade of brown."

"Hmm. . .guess it all depends on the strength of the coffee how dark the stain might be."

He nodded. "Exactly. So, I was thinking maybe you could try using old coffee to paint with. I've got some brushes I could let you have."

Kelly considered his offer carefully. It did sound feasible, but she wouldn't feel right about taking the brushes without paying something for them. If Papa had taught her anything, it was not to accept charity.

"How much would the brushes cost?" she asked Mike.

"I just said I'd be happy to give them to you."

She shook her head. "I either pay, or I don't take the brushes."

He shrugged. "I'll let you have three for a nickel. How's that sound?"

She nodded. "It's a deal."

A few minutes later, Kelly was walking out the door with three small paintbrushes, a jar of cold coffee, and an apple for each mule. Mike had insisted the coffee was a day old and he would have to throw it out if she didn't accept it. Kelly decided stale coffee didn't have much value, so she agreed to take it off his hands. The apples she paid for.

"Come back tomorrow and let me know how your new watercolors work out," Mike said.

She smiled and called over her shoulder, "I may have more pictures for you in the mornin'."

CHAPTER 14

That night after Kelly went to her room, she worked with the coffee watercolors. It was the first time she'd ever used a paintbrush, and it took awhile to get the hang of it. But once she did, Kelly found it to be thoroughly enjoyable. She decided to try a little experiment.

In her bare feet, she crept upstairs to the small kitchen area. She knew her folks were both asleep. She could hear Mama's heavy breathing and Papa's deep snoring.

Kelly lifted the lid from the wooden bin where Mama kept a stash of root vegetables. She pulled out a few carrots, two onions, and a large beet. Next, she heated water in the cast-iron kettle on the cookstove. When it reached the boiling point, she placed her vegetables in three separate bowls and poured scalding water over all. One by one Kelly carried the bowls back to her room. She would let them sit overnight, and by morning, she hoped to have colored water in three different shades.

The following day, Herman's leg was no better, and Papa was fit to be tied.

"I'm losin' money just sittin' here," he hollered as he examined the cut on Herman's leg.

Kelly stood by his side, wishing she had some idea what to say.

"Do you know how many boats I've seen goin' up and down the canal?" he bellowed. "Everyone but me is makin' money this week!"

Kelly thought of the little bit of cash she'd made when Mike paid her for those first few drawings. If Papa were really destitute, she would offer to turn the money over to him. That wasn't the case, though. Her dad was tightfisted with his money, and truth be told, he probably had more stashed away than Kelly would ever see in her lifetime. Besides, she didn't want Papa to know she had any money. If he found out, he would most likely demand that she give it all to him—and any future money she made as well.

So Kelly quietly listened to her father's tirade. He would soon calm down. He always did.

"Should I check with Mike Cooper and see if he has any other medicine that might work better on Herman's cut?" she asked when Papa finally quit blustering.

His face turned bright red, and his forehead wrinkled. "I ain't givin' that man one more dime to take care of an injury that he caused in the first place. We'll sit tight another day and see how Herman's doin' come morning." Papa turned and stomped off toward the boat.

Kelly's Chance

Kelly reached up to stroke Herman behind his ear. "He's a stubborn one, that papa of mine," she mumbled. Yes, they were losing time and money by waiting for the mule's leg to heal, but didn't Papa realize if he spent a little more on medicine, Herman's leg would probably heal faster? Then they could be on their way to Mauch Chunk and be making money that much sooner. Papa was just being mulish.

Kelly dipped her hand into the deep apron pocket where she kept her drawing tablet. At least one good thing had happened this morning. She'd gotten up early and painted a couple of pictures, using her homemade watercolors. The first one was another pose of the mules, only now they were coffee colored, not black. The second picture was of a sunset, with pink, orange, and yellow hues, all because of her vegetable watercolors. She was proud of her accomplishment and could hardly wait to show the pictures to Mike.

"I think I'll head over to his store right

165

now," Kelly said, giving Hector a pat, so he wouldn't feel left out. The mule brayed and nudged her affectionately. Herman and Hector really were her best friends.

A short time later, Kelly entered Mike's store. He was busy waiting on a customer—Mrs. Harris, one of the lock tenders' wives. Kelly waited patiently over by the candy counter. It was tempting to spend some of her money on more lemon drops, but she reminded herself that she still had a few pieces of candy tucked safely away inside the trunk at the foot of her bed. She would wait until those were gone before she considered buying any more.

"Can I help you with something?" Lost in her thoughts, Kelly hadn't realized Mike had finished with his customer and now stood at her side. She drew in a deep breath as the fresh scent of soap reminded her of Mike's presence. He always smelled so clean and unsullied. His nearness sent unwanted tingles along her spine, and she forced herself to keep from trembling.

"I wanted to see what you thought of these." Kelly held out her drawing tablet to Mike.

He studied the first painting of Herman and Hector, done with coffee water. "Hmm. . . not bad. Not bad at all." Then he turned to the next page, and his mouth fell open. "Kelly, how did you make such beautiful colors?"

She giggled, feeling suddenly self-conscious. "I poured boiling water over some carrots, onions, and a beet; then I let it stand all night. This mornin', I had some colored water to paint with."

Mike grinned from ear to ear. "That's really impressive. I'm proud of you, Kelly."

Proud of me? Had she heard Mike right? In all her seventeen years, Kelly didn't remember anyone ever saying they were proud of anything she'd done. She felt the heat of a blush creep up her neck and flood her entire face. "It was nothin' so special."

"Oh, but it was," Mike insisted. "My idea of using coffee water was okay, and your picture of the mules is good, but you took it even further by coming up with a way to make more colors." He lifted the drawing tablet. "You've captured a sunset beautifully."

She smiled, basking in his praise. If only Mama and Papa would say things to encourage her the way Mike did. Mama said very little, and Papa either yelled or criticized.

"I think I'll come up with a better way to display your artwork," Mike announced.

"Oh? What's that?"

"I'm going to make a wooden frame for each of your pictures, and then I'll hang them right there." He pointed to the wall directly behind the counter where he waited on customers. "Nobody will leave my store without first seeing your talented creations."

Talented creations? First Mike had said he was proud of her, and now he'd called her talented. It was almost too much for Kelly to accept. Did he really mean those things, or was he only trying to be nice because he felt sorry for her? She hoped it wasn't the latter, for she didn't want anyone's pity.

"Kelly, did you hear what I said?"

She jerked her head toward Mike. "What did ya say?"

"I asked if you thought framing the pictures would be a good idea."

She nodded. "I suppose so. It's worth a try if you want to go to all that trouble."

"I like working with my hands, so it won't be any trouble at all." Mike looked down at the tablet he still held. "Mind if I take the two colored pictures out now?"

"It's fine by me," she replied, feeling a sense of excitement. "If we stay around here another day or so, maybe I can get a few more drawings done."

He smiled and moved toward the counter. Kelly followed. "That would be great. I hope you do stay around a bit longer—for more reasons than one."

Mike felt such exuberance over Kelly's new

pictures done on newsprint, not to mention the news of her staying for another day or so. He'd been asking God to give him the chance to get to know Kelly better, and it looked as if he might get that opportunity. But he did feel bad that her father was losing money because of the mule's leg. If there was some way he could offer financial assistance, he would, but Mike knew it wouldn't be appreciated. Amos McGregor was a proud man. He'd made that abundantly clear on several occasions.

"Guess I should get goin'," Kelly announced. "Papa left me to tend Herman's leg, and that was some time ago. He'll probably come a-lookin' for me if I don't get back to the boat pretty soon."

Mike carefully removed Kelly's finished pictures and handed her the tablet. "Keep up the good work, and when you get more paintings done, bring them into the store." He chuckled. "If you give me enough, I'll line every wall with your artwork. Then folks won't have any choice but to notice. And if they notice, they're bound to buy."

Kelly snickered, and her face turned crimson. "I like you, Mike Cooper." With that, she turned around and bounded out the door.

Mike flopped down on his wooden stool. "She likes me. Kelly actually said she likes me."

CHAPTER 15

It took three days before Herman's leg was well enough so he could walk without limping. Even then, Papa had said at breakfast that they'd be taking it slow and easy. "No use pushin' things," he told Kelly and her mother. "Wouldn't want Herman to reinjure his leg."

As Kelly connected the towline to the mules' harnesses, a sense of sadness washed over her soul. These last few days had been so nice, being in one place all the time, visiting with Mike

Cooper whenever she had the chance, and painting pictures. She'd used up all her homemade watercolors and would need to make more soon. Kelly figured as she journeyed up the towpath she might come across some plants, tree bark, or leaves she could steep in hot water to make other colors. It would be an adventure to see how many hues she could come up with.

"You all set?" Papa called from the boat.

Kelly waved in response, her signal that she was ready to go. She'd only taken a few steps when she heard someone holler, "Kelly, hold up a minute, would you?"

She whirled around. Mike Cooper was heading her way, holding something in his hands.

Kelly stopped the mules, but Papa shouted at her to get them going again. She knew she'd better keep on walking or suffer the consequences. "I've gotta go," she announced when Mike caught up to her. "Papa's anxious to head out."

"I'll walk with you a ways," he said.

"What about your store?"

"I haven't opened for the day yet."

Kelly clicked her tongue, and the mules moved forward. Then she turned to face Mike as she moved along. The item he held in his hand was a wooden picture frame, and inside was her sunset watercolor.

"What do you think?" Mike asked as she looked at the piece of artwork.

"You did a fine job makin' that frame."

He laughed. "The frame's nothing compared to the beauty of your picture, but it does show off your work really well, don't you think?"

Kelly nodded but kept on walking. If she stopped, the mules would, too.

"When do you think you'll be coming by my store again?" Mike asked.

She shrugged her shoulders. "Can't say for sure. Since Papa lost so much time because of his cough and Herman's leg gettin' cut, he probably won't make any stops that aren't absolutely necessary."

"Guess we could always pray he knocks a

few more bars of soap overboard."

Kelly snickered. "With the way things have been goin' these days, Papa would probably expect me to jump in the canal and fetch 'em back out."

Mike reached out and touched Kelly's arm. She felt a jolt and wondered if he had, too.

"I'm sorry you have to work so hard, Kelly," he murmured.

She nodded and kept moving forward. "I'm used to it, but someday, when I make enough money of my own, I won't be Papa's slave no more."

"I'm sure he doesn't see you as his slave."

She snorted. "I don't get paid for walkin' the mules. Not one single penny had I ever made 'til you sold my two drawings." She glanced at Mike out of the corner of her eye and noticed his shocked expression.

"That will change," he said with a note of conviction. "By the time you stop at my store again, I'm sure several more of your pictures will be gone."

They were coming to a bend in the canal, and Kelly and the mules would be tromping across the changing bridge soon. Kelly knew it was time to tell Mike good-bye, although she hated to see him go. She was beginning to see Mike Cooper as a friend.

"Guess I'd better head back and open up the store," Mike said, "but I wanted to ask you something before you crossed to the other side."

"Oh? What's that?"

"I was wondering if you've ever accepted Christ as your personal Savior. You know— asked Him to forgive your sins and come live in your heart?"

"I did that when I was twelve years old," she said as a lump formed in her throat. Why was Mike asking about her relationship to God, and why was she getting all choked up over a simple good-bye? She'd be seeing Mike again; she just didn't know when.

Mike took hold of Kelly's hand and gave it a gentle squeeze. She glanced back at the boat, hoping Papa couldn't see what was going on.

"I'm awful glad to hear you're a believer. See you soon, Kelly," he whispered.

"I hope so," Kelly said; then she hurried on.

Mike stood watching Kelly until she and the mules disappeared around the bend. She looked so forlorn when they parted. Was she going to miss him as much as he would miss her? He hoped so. These last few days had been wonderful, with her popping into the store a couple of times and the two of them meeting outside on several occasions. Mike felt as though he were beginning to know Kelly better, and he liked what he'd discovered. Not only was the young woman a talented artist, but she was clever. She had figured out how to make her own watercolors, and Mike had a hunch she would probably have come up with even more colors by the time he saw her again.

"Sure hope I've sold some of her artwork by then," he muttered as he turned toward his store. "I can't keep buying them myself, and I wouldn't want Kelly to find out about the two I did pay for."

An image of Kelly lying on the patchwork quilt they'd used at the Sunday picnic flashed across Mike's mind. If Betsy hadn't been there, he might have taken a chance and kissed his sleeping beauty, for he was quickly losing his heart to Kelly McGregor.

Kelly had to hold up the mules at the changing bridge, as two other boats passed and their mules went over. While she waited, she decided to take advantage of the time, so she reached into her apron pocket and pulled out her drawing pad and a stick of charcoal. Kelly had just begun to sketch the boat ahead of her when Reverend Nelson and his daughter came walking up the towpath.

"Good morning," the preacher said. "It's a fine day, wouldn't you say?"

Kelly nodded in reply.

"Daddy and I are walking a stretch of the towpath today," Betsy remarked. "We're calling at people's homes who live near the canal, as well as visiting with those we meet along the way." She stuck out her hand and waved a piece of paper in front of Kelly's face. "We're handing these out. Would you like one?"

"What is it?" Kelly asked.

"It's a verse of scripture," Reverend Nelson answered before his daughter could respond.

Kelly took the Bible verse with a mumbled thanks, then stuffed it into her apron pocket. She would look at it later.

"What's that you're drawing?" the pastor asked.

"One of the canal boats."

Reverend Nelson glanced at her tablet and smiled. "It's a good likeness."

Kelly shrugged her shoulders. "I've only just begun."

"Betsy has one of your drawings. It's quite well done, considering what you have to work with."

Wanda E. Brunstetter

Kelly's mouth dropped open. Betsy had one of her drawings? But how? A light suddenly dawned. The preacher's daughter must have gone into Mike's store and purchased one of Kelly's pictures. She smiled at Betsy and asked, "Which one did you buy?"

Betsy's pale eyebrows drew together as she frowned. "The picture is of a couple children fishing on the canal, but I didn't buy it."

"You didn't?"

Betsy shook her head. "Mike Cooper gave it to me as a birthday present. A few weeks ago he came over to our house for supper and to help me celebrate. He presented it to me then."

Kelly felt as though someone had punched her in the stomach. If Mike had given one of the drawings away, then he must have bought it himself. Her fingers coiled tightly around the piece of charcoal she still held in her hand. Who had bought the other picture Mike had paid her for? Was it him? He hadn't actually said so, but he'd given her the impression that he'd sold the pictures to some customers who'd come into the store.

The ground beneath her feet began to rumble as a steam train lumbered past. Billows of smoke from the burning coal poured into the sky, leaving a dark, sooty trail.

"Guess we'd better be moving on," the preacher said with a wave of his hand.

Kelly nodded. Her heart was hammering in her chest like the *clickety-clack* of the train's wheels against the track.

Just wait until I drop by Mike's store again, she fumed. *I'm gonna give that man a piece of my mind, and that's for certain sure!*

For the rest of the day Kelly fretted about the pictures Mike had supposedly sold. At supper that night, she was in a sour mood and didn't feel much like eating, even though Mama had made Irish stew, a favorite with both Kelly and her dad.

"What was that storekeeper doing,

walkin' along the towpath with you this mornin'?" Papa asked, sending Kelly a disgruntled look.

She shrugged and switched her focus to the bowl of stew in front of her. "He was showin' me something he made and plans to sell in his store."

"What did he make?" Mama questioned.

Kelly had hoped neither of her parents would question her further. She didn't want them to know she'd given Mike some of her drawings and paintings to sell in his store. And she sure wasn't about to tell them the storekeeper had been the only person to buy any of her work.

"It was a picture frame," she said, her mind searching for anything she could say to change the subject. She took a bite of stew and smacked her lips. "This is delicious, Mama. Good as always."

Her mother smiled from ear to ear. She was a good cook; there was no denying it. Mama could take a few vegetables and a slab of dried meat and turn it into a nutritious, tasty meal.

"I don't want that storekeeper hangin' around you, Kelly. Is that understood?"

At the sound of her dad's threatening voice, Kelly dropped the spoon, and it landed in her bowl, splashing stew broth all over the oilcloth table covering.

"You don't have to shout, Amos," Mama said in her usual soft-spoken tone.

"I'll shout whenever I feel like it," he shot back, giving Kelly's mother a mind-your-own-business look.

Mama quickly lowered her gaze, but Kelly, feeling braver than usual, spoke her mind. "Mike and I are just friends. I don't see what harm there is in us havin' a conversation once in a while."

"Humph!" Papa sputtered. "From what I could see, the two of you was havin' more than a little talk."

So he had seen Mike take her hand. Kelly trembled, but she couldn't let her father know how flustered she felt. She was glad Mama hadn't said anything about her and Mike going on a picnic together, for that would surely get Papa riled.

Mama touched Kelly's arm. "I think your dad is concerned that you'll run off with some man, the way Sarah did."

"You needn't worry about that," Kelly was quick to say. "I don't plan on ever gettin' married." *Besides, Mike Cooper's not interested in me. It's Betsy Nelson he's set his cap for.*

"I'm glad to hear that." Papa tapped his knife along the edge of the table. "Just so you know, if I catch that storekeeper with his hands on you again, I'll knock his block off. Is that clear enough?"

Kelly nodded, as her eyes filled with tears. She might be mad as all get-out at Mike, but she couldn't stand to think of him getting beat up by her dad. She would have to make sure Mike never touched her when Papa was around. Not that she wanted him to, of course.

She reached into her pocket for a hanky and found the slip of paper Betsy Nelson had given her instead. Holding it in her lap, so Papa couldn't see it, Kelly silently read the verse of Scripture: *"Jesus said, 'If ye forgive men their trespasses, your heavenly Father will also forgive you' " Matthew 6:14.*

Kelly swallowed hard. She knew she needed to forgive Papa for the way he acted toward her. It sure wouldn't be easy, though.

CHAPTER 16

On Thursday morning, a sack of mail was delivered to Mike's store, brought in by one of the canal boats. This was a weekly occurrence, as Mike's place of business also served as the area's post office.

While sorting through the pile of letters and packages, Mike discovered one addressed to him. He recognized his brother Alvin's handwriting and quickly tore open the envelope.

Kelly's Chance

Mike hadn't heard from either Alvin or John in several months, so he was anxious to see what the letter had to say:

> Dear Mike,
>
> John and me are both fine, and our fishing business is doing right well. I wanted to let you know that I've found myself a girlfriend, and we plan to be married in December, when we'll be done fishing for the season.
>
> Hope things are good for you there at the store.
>
> Your brother,
> Alvin

Mike was happy for his brother, but he couldn't help feeling a pang of envy. He wanted so much to have a wife and children, and he wasn't any closer to it now than he had been several weeks before, when he'd prayed earnestly for God to send him a wife. He was still hoping Kelly McGregor might be that woman, but so far, she'd given him no indication that she was interested in anything beyond friendship. At least he knew she had a personal relationship with Christ, even though she had been in a hurry when he'd asked her so they couldn't really discuss it.

Mike turned and glanced at the wall directly behind the counter. He'd framed all of Kelly's pictures and hung them there. One had sold yesterday, and the man who'd bought it seemed interested in the others. No doubt Kelly had talent, but she was also young and probably insecure when it came to men. Maybe she didn't know how to show her feelings. Maybe she was afraid. Mike had noticed how Amos McGregor often yelled at Kelly and his wife. Kelly might think all men were like her dad.

"I'll go slow with Kelly and win her heart over time," Mike murmured as he continued to study her artwork. "And while I'm waiting, I'll try even harder to get some of these pictures sold."

[object Object]# Kelly's Chance

Papa had kept true to his word and taken it slow and easy on the trip to Mauch Chunk. On a normal run, they would have been there by Wednesday night. Instead, they'd spent Wednesday night outside the small town of Parryville.

They arrived in Mauch Chunk on Thursday afternoon, with Herman doing well and his leg in good shape. Then they loaded the boat with coal from the loading chutes, which descended 250 feet to the river. They spent the night in Mauch Chunk, surrounded by hills that were covered with birch, maple, oak, and wild locust trees.

The next morning, they were heading back toward Easton to deliver their load. They'd be passing Mike's store either that evening or the next morning, depending on how hard Papa pushed. Since Herman was doing well, Kelly suspected they would move faster than they had on Wednesday and Thursday.

"Probably won't be stopping at Mike's store this time," Kelly mumbled. "Sure wish we were, though. I need to talk to him about the picture he gave Betsy Nelson."

As the wind whipped against her long skirt, Kelly glanced up at the darkening sky. They were in for a storm, sure as anything. She hoped it would hold off until they stopped for the night. She hated walking the towpath during a rainstorm.

Hector's ears twitched, as though he sensed the impending danger a torrential downpour could cause—fallen trees, a muddy towpath, rising canal waters. And there was always the threat of being hit by lightning, especially with so many trees lining the path. A few years back, a young boy leading his dad's mules had been struck by a bolt of lightning and was killed instantly.

Kelly shivered. Just thinking about what was to come made her feel jumpy as a frog. The mules would be harder to handle once the rain started because they had no depth perception and hated walking through water, even small puddles. If they came to a stretch of puddles, they would tromp clear around them. There was no fear of the mules jumping into the canal to get cooled off on a hot day the way a horse would have done. Kelly's mules liked water for drinking, but that was all.

Forcing her mind off the impending storm, Kelly thought about how glad she was that Papa had chosen mules, not horses, to pull his boats. It was a proven fact that mules, with their brute strength and surefooted agility, were much less skittish and far more reliable than any horse could be. If horses weren't stopped in time, they would keep on pulling until they fell over dead. Mules, if they were overly tired or had fallen sick, would stop in the middle of the path and refuse to budge. A mule ate one-third less food than a horse did as well, making the beast of burden far more economical.

By noon, rain began falling. First it arrived in tiny droplets, splattering the end of Kelly's nose. Then the lightning and thunder came, bringing a chilling downpour.

Kelly cupped her hands around her mouth and leaned into the wind. "Are we gonna stop soon?" she hollered to Papa, who stood at the stern of the boat, already dripping wet. He was just getting over a bad cold and shouldn't be out in this weather.

"Keep movin'!" Papa shouted back to her. "We won't stop unless it gets worse."

Worse? Kelly didn't see how it could get much worse. Thunder rumbled across the sky, and black clouds hung so low she felt as if she could touch them. "I–I'm cold and wet," she yelled, wondering if he could hear her. The wind was howling fiercely, and she could barely hear herself. Then Kelly's straw hat flew off her head, causing long strands of hair to blow across her face. She ran up ahead, retrieved the hat, and pushed it down on her head, hoping it would stay in place.

Papa leaned over the edge of the boat and tossed a jacket over the side. Kelly lunged forward and barely caught it in time. If it had fallen into the canal, it would have been lost forever, as the murky brown water was swirling and gurgling something awful.

Kelly slipped her arms into the oversized wool jacket and buttoned it up to her neck. It helped some to keep out the wind, but she knew it was only a matter of time until the rain leaked through and soaked her clean to the skin.

On and on Kelly and the mules trudged, through the driving rain, pushing against the wind, tromping in and out of mud puddles, murk, and mire. Several times, the mules balked and refused to move forward. Kelly coaxed, pushed, pleaded, and pulled until she finally got them moving again.

By the time Papa signaled her to stop, Kelly felt like a limp dishrag. She glanced around and realized they were directly in front of Mike's store. Lifting her gaze to the thunderous sky, Kelly prayed, "Thank You, God, for keepin' us safe and for givin' Papa the good sense to stop."

"We're stayin' here for the night," Papa shouted. "Help me get the mules on board the boat."

"Can't they bed down in Mike Cooper's barn tonight?" Kelly asked. "I could care for 'em better there."

"Guess it wouldn't hurt for one night," Papa surprised her by saying.

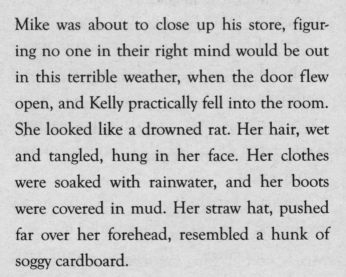

Mike was about to close up his store, figuring no one in their right mind would be out in this terrible weather, when the door flew open, and Kelly practically fell into the room. She looked like a drowned rat. Her hair, wet and tangled, hung in her face. Her clothes were soaked with rainwater, and her boots were covered in mud. Her straw hat, pushed far over her forehead, resembled a hunk of soggy cardboard.

Mike grabbed hold of Kelly as a gust of wind pushed her forward. The door slammed shut with so much force that the broom, lying against one wall, toppled over, while several pieces of paper blew off the counter and sailed to the floor.

"Kelly, what are you doing here?" he questioned.

"We've stopped for the day because of the storm." She leaned into him, and he had the sudden desire to kiss her. Why was it that every time they were together anymore, Mike wanted to find out what her lips would feel like against his own?

He drew in a deep breath and gently stroked her back. "Are you okay? You look miserable."

She pulled away. "I'm fine, but we were wonderin' if we could stable the mules in your barn tonight."

He nodded. "Of course. I'll put on my jacket and help you get them settled in."

"I can manage," she said in a brisk tone of voice. She'd been so friendly a few minutes ago. What had happened to make her change?

Mike studied Kelly's face. It was pinched,

and tears streamed down her face. At least he thought they were tears. They might have been raindrops.

"Kelly, what's wrong?" Mike touched her arm, and she recoiled as if some pesky insect had bitten her.

As she moved toward the door, her gaze swung to the pictures on the wall.

"How do you like the way I've got your artwork displayed?" he questioned.

She squinted her eyes at him. "How could you, Mike?"

"How could I what?"

"Buy my drawing and give it to Betsy Nelson for her birthday?"

"Her dad invited me to their house for supper to help her celebrate. I wanted to take something, and I thought Betsy would like one of your wonderful charcoal drawings."

She continued to stare at him, and Mike felt his face heat up. Why was she looking at him as though he'd done something wrong? He'd paid her for the picture; same as if someone else had bought it.

"And the other drawing?"

"Huh?"

"You gave me money for two drawings and said you'd sold them both."

The heat Mike felt on his face had now spread to his ears. "I. . .that is. . .I bought both of the pictures," he admitted. "One for Betsy's birthday and the other to hang in my living room."

She shook her head slowly. "I figured as much."

"How did you find out about the picture I gave the preacher's daughter?"

"Reverend Nelson told me when I ran into him and Betsy on the towpath the other day." Kelly bit down on her lower lip, like she might be about to cry. "Why'd ya lead me to believe you'd sold my pictures, Mike?"

"I did sell them," he defended. "I don't see what difference it makes who bought them."

"It makes a lot of difference," Kelly shouted

before she turned toward the front door. "I may be poor but I don't need charity from you or anyone else!"

He couldn't let her leave like this. Not without making her understand he wasn't trying to hurt her. Mike grabbed Kelly's arm and turned her around. "Please forgive me. I never meant to upset you, and I really did want those drawings." He pointed to the wall where her other paintings hung. "I sold one of your watercolors this morning to a man who lives in Walnutport."

She squinted her dark eyes at him. "Really?"

"Yes. He was impressed with your work and said he may be back to buy more."

Kelly's eyes were swimming with tears. "I—I can't believe it."

"It's true. Mr. Porter knows talent when he sees it, and so do I." Mike reached for her hand and gave it a gentle squeeze. "Am I forgiven for misleading you?"

She hesitated a moment, then her lips curved up. "Yes."

"Good. Now will you let me help you stable the mules?"

She nodded.

Mike grabbed his jacket off the wall peg by the door. "You lead one mule, and I'll take the other."

A moment later, they stepped into the driving rain, but Mike paid it no mind. All he could think about was spending the next hour or so in the company of Kelly McGregor.

CHAPTER 17

———————❋———————

During the next half hour, Kelly and Mike got the mules fed and bedded down for the night. Kelly was grateful for his help and the loan of the barn. It meant Herman and Hector had a warm, dry place to rest, without the bouncing and swaying from the rough waters caused by the storm.

Truth be told, Kelly dreaded going to her own room. It would be hard to sleep with the boat bobbing all over the place. She'd probably have to tie herself in bed in order to keep from being tossed onto the floor.

"I was wondering if you and your folks would like to stay at my place tonight," Mike said, as he rubbed Herman down with an old towel.

"Your place?"

"My house. I've got plenty of room."

Kelly wondered if Mike had been able to read her mind. Or was he smart enough to figure out how difficult it would be to spend the night on a boat riding the waves of a storm?

"I'd have to ask Papa and Mama," she said. "They might agree, but I'm not sure."

"Would you prefer it if I asked them instead?"

"That probably would be best. Papa's usually more open to things if it comes from someone other than me."

Mike hung the towel on a nail and moved toward Kelly, who'd been drying Hector off with a piece of heavy cloth. "I take it you and your pa don't get along."

Kelly lowered her gaze to the wooden floor. "I used to think he liked me well enough, but ever since Sarah left, he's been actin' meaner than ever."

Mike's heart clenched. He hated to see the way Kelly's shoulders drooped or hear the resignation in her voice. "Are you afraid of him, Kelly?"

She nodded slowly. "Sometimes."

"Has he ever hit you?"

"Not since I was little. Then it was only a swat on the backside." Kelly's eyes filled with tears, and it was all Mike could do to keep from kissing her. "Papa mostly yells, but sometimes he makes me do things I know are wrong."

"Like what?"

She sucked in her lower lip. "The other day, a bunch of chickens was runnin' around near the towpath. He insisted I grab hold of one and give it to Mama to cook for our supper that night."

Mike drew in a deep breath and let it out in a rush. "But that's stealing. Doesn't your dad know taking things that don't belong to you is breaking one of God's commandments?"

"Papa don't care about God. He thinks Mama is plain silly for readin' her Bible every night."

"What do you think would have happened if you'd refused to do what your dad asked?"

"I don't know, but I didn't think I should find out."

Mike could hardly believe Kelly's dad had asked her to do something so wrong, but it was equally hard to understand why she wouldn't stand up to him. If he didn't threaten her physically, what kind of hold did the man have on her?

"Does your dad refuse to pay you if you don't do what he asks?" Mike questioned.

Kelly planted her hands on her hips. "I told you the other day, Papa has never paid me a single penny for leadin' the mules."

Mike reached up to scratch the side of his head. He'd forgotten about their conversation about Kelly's lack of money. That was why she wanted to sell some of her artwork. And it was one more reason Mike had to help make it happen.

"It's all Sarah's fault for runnin' off with one of the lock tender's sons. She made Papa angry and left me with all the work." Kelly balled her fingers into tight fists, and Mike wondered if she might want to punch someone. He took a few steps back, just in case.

Before he had a chance to respond to her tirade, Kelly announced, "I'm afraid men are all the same, and I ain't never gettin' married, that's for certain sure!"

Mike felt like he'd been kicked in the gut. Never marry? Had he heard her right? If Kelly was dead-set against marriage, what hope did he have of winning her hand? About all he could do was try to be her friend, but he sure wished he could figure out some way to prove to her that all men weren't like her dad.

Kelly felt the heat of embarrassment flood her

face. What had possessed her to spout off like that in front of Mike? He'd been helping her with the mules and sure didn't deserve such wrath. She knew she should apologize, but the words stuck in her throat.

She grabbed a hunk of hay and fed it to Hector. Maybe if she kept her hands busy, she wouldn't have to think about anything else.

"Why don't you finish up with the mules while I go talk to your folks and see if they'd like to spend the night at my place?" Mike suggested.

Kelly nodded. "Sounds good to me."

She heard the barn door close behind Mike, and she dropped to her knees. "Oh, Lord, I'm sorry for bein' such a grouch. Guess I'm just tired and out of sorts tonight 'cause of the storm and all."

Tears streamed down Kelly's cheeks. Mike thought she was a sinner for taking that chicken. He didn't understand how things were with Papa, either. To make matters worse, Mike had been kind to her, and she'd yelled at him in return. What must he think of her now?

"I'm sorry for stealin' the chicken, Lord. Give me the courage to tell Papa no from now on."

Kelly dried her eyes with the backs of her hands and was about to leave the barn when Mike showed up with Mama.

"Where's Papa?" Kelly questioned.

Her mother sighed deeply. "He's bound and determined to stay on the boat tonight. Never mind that it's rockin' back and forth like a bucking mule." She wrinkled her nose. "And now the roof's leaking as well."

"So are you and me gonna stay at Mike's house?" Kelly asked.

"Yes, and it was a very kind offer, wouldn'tcha say?"

Kelly nodded in response and smiled at Mike. "Sorry for snappin' like a turtle."

He winked at her. "Apology accepted."

For the next two days, the storm continued, and Papa refused to leave the boat. He said he might lose it if he did, but Kelly knew the truth. Her dad didn't want to appear needy in front of Mike. He'd rather sit on his vessel and be tossed about like a chunk of wood thrown into a raging river than accept anyone's charity.

Sitting at Mike's kitchen table with her drawing tablet, Kelly thought about Proverbs 12:27, a verse of scripture she'd learned as a child: *"The substance of a diligent man is precious."* Papa was diligent, that was for sure. Too bad he wasn't kinder or more concerned about his family.

The last two nights, she and Mama had shared a bed inside a real home, and Kelly found herself wishing even more that she could leave the life of a mule driver behind.

"Aren't you gonna eat some breakfast?" Mama asked, pushing a bowl of oatmeal in front of Kelly.

"I will, after I finish this drawing."

Mama leaned forward with her elbows on the table. "What are you makin'?"

"It's a picture of our boat bein' tossed by

the rising waters. I took a walk down to the canal this morning so I could see how things were lookin'." Kelly frowned. "The rain hasn't let up one little bit, and I figure God must be awful angry with someone."

Mama looked at Kelly as if she'd taken leave of her senses. "What would make ya say somethin' like that?"

"Doesn't God cause the rain and winds to come whenever He's mad?"

Reaching across the table, Mama took hold of Kelly's hand. "Storms are part of the world we live in, but I don't believe God sends 'em to make us pay for our sins."

"Really?"

Mama nodded. "The Bible tells us in Psalm 34:19, 'Many are the afflictions of the righteous: but the Lord delivereth him out of them all.' Everyone goes through trials, and some of those come in the form of storms, sickness, or other such things. That don't mean we're bein' punished, but we can have the assurance that even though we'll have afflictions, God will deliver us in His time."

Kelly tried to concentrate on her drawing, but Mama's words kept rolling around in her head. *When's my time comin' to be delivered, Lord? When are You gonna give me enough money so I can leave this terrible way of life?*

She grabbed the hunk of charcoal and continued to draw, not wanting to think about her situation. It was bad enough that the storm wasn't letting up and Papa refused to get off the boat. She didn't wish to spend the rest of the day worried about God's direction for her life. If more of her drawings didn't sell soon, she'd have to figure out some other way to make money on her own. When they wintered in Easton, Kelly might get a job in one of the factories. Then she'd have plenty of money, and Papa could find someone else to lead the mules.

A few minutes later, the door flew open, and Papa lumbered into the room. Mama jumped up and moved quickly toward him.

"Oh, Amos, it's so good to see you. Can

I fix ya a bowl of oatmeal or maybe some flapjacks?"

He stormed right past Mama as though she hadn't said a word about food. "Stupid weather! It ain't bad enough we lost so much time with sickness and mule problems; now we're stuck here 'til the storm passes by. I'm gettin' sick of sittin' around doin' nothin', and I can't believe my family abandoned me to come get all cozy-like over here at the storekeeper's place!"

Kelly tried to ignore her dad's outburst, but it was hard, especially with him breathing down her neck, as he was now. She could feel his hot breath against her cheek, as he leaned his head close to the table. "What's that you're doin'?" he snarled.

"I'm drawin' a picture of our boat in the storm."

"Humph! Ain't it bad enough I have to endure the torment of bein' tossed around like a cork? Do ya have to rub salt in the wounds by makin' a dumb picture to remind me of my plight?"

Kelly's Chance

Kelly opened her mouth to reply, but Papa jerked the piece of paper right off the table. "This is trash and deserves to be treated as such!" With that, he marched across the room, flung open the door on the woodstove, and tossed Kelly's picture into the fire.

She shot out of her seat, but it was too late. Angry flames of red had already engulfed her precious drawing.

"How could you, Papa?" she cried. "How could you be so cruel?" Kelly rushed from the house, not caring that she wasn't wearing a jacket.

CHAPTER 18

Mike glanced out the store window and was surprised to see Kelly run past. She wasn't wearing a jacket, and the rain was still pouring down. She would be drenched within seconds.

He yanked the door open and hurried out after her. She raced into the barn, and Mike was right behind her.

"Kelly, what are you doing out here without a coat?" he hollered as he followed her into the mules' stall.

She kept her head down, and he could see her shoulders shaking.

Mike rushed over to her. "What's wrong? Why are you crying?"

She lifted her gaze to his, her dark eyes filled with tears. He ached to hold her in his arms—to kiss away those tears. He might have, too, if he hadn't been afraid of her response.

"I was working on a drawing of our boat this mornin', and Papa got mad and threw it into the fire," she sobbed.

Mike took hold of Kelly's arms. "Why would he do such a thing?"

"He stormed into your kitchen, yelled about the weather, and said I was rubbin' salt into his wounds by makin' a picture of the boat in the storm. Then he said my picture was trash and deserved to be treated as such. That's when he turned it to ashes." Tears streamed down Kelly's face, and Mike instinctively reached up to wipe them away with the back of his hand.

"I'm so sorry, Kelly. I promise someday things will be better for you."

"How can you say that? Are you able to see into the future and know what's ahead?" she wailed.

Mike shook his head slowly. Kelly was right; he couldn't be sure what the future held for either of them. He wanted things to be better and wished she would allow him to love her and help her. If Kelly were to marry him, Mike would gladly spend the rest of his life taking care of her. If only he felt free to tell her that.

"God loves you, Kelly, and He wants only the best for you."

She glared up at him. "If God loves me so much, then why do I have to work long hours with no pay? And why's Papa so mean?"

"God gives each of us a free will, and your dad is the way he is by his own choosing. We can pray for him and set a good example, but nobody can make him change until he's ready."

Kelly sniffed deeply. "I don't care if he ever changes. All I care about is earnin' enough money to make it on my own. I need that chance, so if you want to pray about somethin', then ask God to help *me*."

Mike's hand rested comfortably on her shoulder. With only a slight pull, she would be close enough for him to kiss. The urge was nearly overwhelming, and he moved away, fighting for control. Kelly had made clear how she felt about marriage. Even if she were attracted to him—and he suspected she was—they had no hope of a future together. He wanted marriage and children so much. All she seemed to care about was drawing pictures and making money so she could support herself. Didn't Kelly realize he was more than willing to care for her needs? As long as he was able to draw breath, Mike would never let his wife or children do without.

"I'll be praying, Kelly," he mumbled. "Praying for both you and your dad."

The following Monday, the rain finally stopped, and the canal waters had receded enough so the McGregors could move on. Kelly felt a deep sense of sadness as she said good-bye to Mike. He truly was her friend, and as much as she hated to admit it, she was attracted to him. She would miss their daily chats as she cared for the mules. She would miss his kind words and caring attitude. As the days of summer continued, she hoped they would stop by his store on a regular basis—not only to see if any of her paintings had sold, but also so she could spend more time with Mike.

With Mike's encouragement over the last few days, she'd done several more charcoal drawings, always out of Papa's sight.

"Get up there," Kelly said as she coaxed the mules to get going. They moved forward, and she turned to wave at Mike one last time. She didn't know why she should feel so sad. She'd see him again, probably on their return trip from Easton.

They'd only traveled a short ways when Papa signaled her to stop. They were between towns, and no other boats were around. She had a sinking feeling her dad was up to something. Something he'd done a few times before when he'd lost time due to bad weather or some kind of mishap along the way.

Sure enough, within minutes of their stopping, Papa had begun to shovel coal out of the compartment where it was stored and was dumping it into the canal. He did this to lighten their load, which in turn would help the boat move faster. Of course, it also meant Kelly would be expected to keep the mules moving at a quicker pace.

She shook her head in disgust. "I don't see why Papa has to be so dishonest."

Hector brayed loudly, as though he agreed.

"It's not fair for him to expect the three of us to walk faster," she continued to fume. "It's hard enough to walk at a regular pace, what with the mud and all, but now we'll practically have to run."

Kelly's thoughts took her back to what Mike had told her the other morning in his barn. He'd said they needed to pray for Kelly's dad and set him a good example. That was a tall order—especially since Papa seemed determined to be ornery and didn't think twice about cheating someone. She knew from experience that, shortly before they arrived in Easton to deliver their load, Papa would wet the coal down, making it weigh more. Since he was paid by weight and not by the amount, no one would be any the wiser.

She sighed deeply and turned her head away from the canal. There was no use watching what she couldn't prevent happening. Someday, maybe she wouldn't have to watch it at all.

For the next several weeks, Kelly trudged up and down the towpath between Easton and Mauch Chunk, but they made no stops that weren't absolutely necessary. Papa said they'd lost enough time, and he didn't think they needed to dally. When Mama complained about needing fresh vegetables, Papa solved the problem by turning the tiller over to her. Then he jumped off the boat and helped himself to some carrots and beets growing near the towpath. The garden belonged to someone who lived nearby, but Papa didn't care. He said if the people who'd planted the vegetables so close to the canal didn't want folks helping themselves, they ought to have fenced in their crops.

Kelly had been praying for Papa, like Mike suggested, but it seemed the more she prayed, the worse he became. The effort appeared to be futile, and she had about decided to give up praying or even hoping Papa might ever change.

That morning at breakfast, Mama had asked Papa if they could stop at Mike's store later in the afternoon. She needed more washing soap, some thread, flour for baking, and a few other things she couldn't get by without. After a few choice words, Papa had finally agreed, but now, as they neared the spot in front of Cooper's General Store, Kelly wondered if he might change his mind. His face was a mask of anger, but he signaled her to stop.

She breathed a sigh of relief and halted the mules. At last she could see Mike again and ask if any of her pictures had sold. She didn't have more to give him. She'd been too busy during the days to draw, and at night, she was too tuckered out. At the rate things were going, Kelly doubted she'd ever get the chance to earn enough money to buy any store-bought paint, much less to open an art gallery.

"A dream. That's all it is," she mumbled moments before Mama joined her to head for the store.

Mike stood behind the front counter, praying and hoping Kelly would stop by his store soon.

He'd just sold another one of her paintings, and he could hardly wait to tell her the good news. It had been two whole weeks since he'd spoken with her, although he had seen the McGregors' boat go by on several occasions. Each time, he'd had customers in the store, or else he would have dashed outside and tried to speak with Kelly—although it probably would have meant running along the towpath as they conversed, for that's pretty much what it looked like Kelly had been doing. Her dad was most likely trying to make up for all the time he'd lost during the storm, but Mike hated to see Kelly being pushed so hard. It wasn't right for a young woman to work from sunup to sunset without getting paid.

Mike was pleasantly surprised when the front door opened and in walked Dorrie and Kelly McGregor. They both looked tired, but Kelly's face showed more than fatigue. Her dark eyes had lost their sparkle, and her shoulders were slumped. She looked defeated.

Mike smiled at the two women. "It's good

to see you. Is there something I can help you with?"

Dorrie waved a hand. "Don't trouble yourself. I can get whatever I'm needin'." She marched off in the direction of the sewing notions.

Kelly hung back, and she lifted her gaze to the wall where her artwork was displayed.

"I sold another picture this morning," Mike announced.

"That's good," she said with little feeling. "Sorry I don't have any more to give you right now. There's been no time for drawin' or paintin' here of late."

"It's all right," he assured her. "I'm sure you'll find some free time soon."

She scowled at him. "Why do you always say things like that?"

"Like what?"

"You try to make me think things are gonna get better when they're not."

"How do you know they're not?"

"I just do, that's all."

Mike blew out his breath. It was obvious nothing he said would penetrate her negative attitude this afternoon. He offered up a quick prayer. *Lord, give me the right words.*

"Would it help if I had a talk with your dad?"

Kelly looked horrified. "Don't you dare! Papa would be furious if he knew I'd been complaining." She squared her shoulders. "I'll be fine, so there's no reason to concern yourself."

"But I am concerned. I'm in—" Mike stopped himself before he blurted out that he was in love with her. He knew it would be the worst thing he could say to Kelly right now. Besides the fact that she was in a sour mood and would probably not appreciate his declaration of love, her mother was in the store and might be listening to his every word.

Mike moved over to the candy counter. "How about a bag of lemon drops? I'm sure you're out of them by now."

Kelly's frown faded, and she joined him at the counter. "Since I sold a painting and have some money comin', I'll take two bags of candy—one lemon drops, and the other horehounds."

"I didn't know you fancied horehounds."

"I don't, but Papa likes 'em. Maybe it'll help put him in a better mood."

So she was trying to set a good example for her dad. At least one of Mike's prayers was being answered. If Kelly's dad found the Lord, then Kelly might be more receptive to the idea of marriage.

Mike reached into the container of horehound drops with a wooden scoop. "You think you might be stopping over come Sunday?"

She shrugged her shoulders. "If we make it to Mauch Chunk in good time, Papa might be willin' to stop on our way back. Why do you ask?"

"I'd like to take you on another picnic." He grinned at her. "Only this time it'll be just you and me."

She tipped her head to one side. "No Betsy Nelson?"

"Nope."

She smiled for the first time since she'd come into the store. "We'll have to wait and see."

CHAPTER 19

❊

When Mike asked Kelly about going on another picnic, she never expected her family's canal boat would be stopped in front of his store the next Sunday. They'd arrived the evening before, and Papa had decided to spend the night so he could work on the boat the following morning. He'd accidentally run into one of the other canal boats and put a hole in the bow of his boat. It wasn't large, and it was high enough that no water had leaked in, but it still needed to be repaired before it got any worse. Papa would be busy with that all day, which meant Kelly could head off with Mike and probably go unnoticed.

Not wishing to run into Betsy again, Kelly waited until the crowd had dispersed from Reverend Nelson's outdoor preaching service before she walked to Mike's store. They'd talked briefly the night before and had agreed to meet sometime after noon in front of his place.

It was a hot summer day in late August, and Kelly wished she and Mike could go swimming in the canal to get cooled off. She dismissed the idea as quickly as it popped into her mind when she remembered Mike had said he didn't swim well, and she, though able to swim, was afraid of water snakes. They would have to find some other way to find solace from the oppressive heat and humidity.

Mike was waiting for her in front of the store, a picnic basket in one hand and a blanket in the other. "Did you bring along your drawing tablet?" he asked.

She nodded and patted the pocket of her long gingham skirt.

"I thought we'd have our picnic at the pond behind Zach Miller's house. There's lots of wildflowers growing there, and maybe we can find some to brew into watercolors," he said, offering Kelly a smile that made her skin tingle despite the heat of the day.

"That would be good. Mama's runnin' low on carrots and beets, so I haven't been able to make any colors for a spell, other than the shades I've gotten from leftover coffee and tree bark."

Mike whistled as they walked up the tow-path, heading in the direction of the lock tender's house.

"You seem to be in an awful good mood this afternoon," Kelly noted.

He turned his head and grinned at her. "I'm always in fine spirits on the Lord's Day. I looked for you at the preaching service but didn't see you anywhere."

"Mama needed my help with some bakin'." Kelly felt a prick of her conscience. She had helped her mother bake oatmeal bread, but truth be told, that wasn't the real reason she hadn't attended the church service. She didn't want to hear God's Word and be reminded that her prayers weren't being answered where Papa was concerned. Besides, Mama hadn't attended church, either, and if she didn't feel the need to go, why should Kelly?

"Sure wish you could have heard the great message the reverend delivered this morning. It was a real inspiration."

"I'm sure it was."

"Summer will be over soon," Mike said, changing the subject. "Won't be long until the leaves begin to turn and drop from the trees."

Kelly nodded, feeling suddenly sad. When fall came, they'd only have a few months left to make coal deliveries. Winter often hit quickly, and Papa always moored the boat for the winter and moved them to Flannigan's Boardinghouse in Easton, where they would live until the spring thaw. That meant Kelly wouldn't be seeing Mike for several months. She would miss his smiling face and their long talks.

A lot could happen in three months. Mike and Betsy might start courting and could even be married by the time they returned to the canal. And Kelly was acutely aware that lots of coal was now being hauled via steam train, which meant fewer boats were working the canals in eastern Pennsylvania. How long would it be before Papa gave up canaling altogether and took a year-round job in the city?

"A lemon drop for your thoughts," Mike said.

"What?"

"I brought along a bag of your favorite candy, and I'd gladly give you one if you're willin' to share your thoughts with me."

She snickered. "I doubt anything I'd be thinkin' would be worth even one lemon drop."

Mike stopped walking and turned to face

her. "Don't say that, Kelly. You're a talented, intelligent woman, and I value anything you might have to say."

She pursed her lips. "I'm not sure 'bout my talents, but one thing I do know—I'm not smart. I've only gone through the eighth grade, and that took me longer than most, 'cause I just attended school during the winter."

"A lack of education doesn't mean you're stupid," Mike said with a note of conviction. "My dad used to say he graduated from the school of life and that all the things he learned helped him become a better man. We grow from our experiences, so if we learn from our mistakes, then we're smart."

Kelly contemplated Mike's words a few seconds. "Hmm. . .I've never thought about it that way before."

"I hope to have a whole passel of kids someday, and when I do, I want to teach them responsibility so they can work hard and be smart where it really counts."

Kelly wasn't sure she liked the sound of

that, but she chose not to comment.

Mike started walking again, and Kelly did as well. Soon they were at the pond behind the Millers' house. Nobody else was around, so Kelly figured they weren't likely to be interrupted, and she might even get some serious drawing done.

Sitting on the blanket next to Kelly, his belly full of fried chicken and buttermilk biscuits, Mike felt content. He could spend the rest of his life with this woman—watching her draw, listening to the hum of her sweet voice, and kissing away all her worries and cares. Should he tell her what he was feeling? Would it scare her off? He drew in a deep breath and plunged ahead. "Kelly, I was wondering—"

"Yes?" she murmured as she continued to draw the outline of a clump of wildflowers.

"Would it be all right if I wrote to you while you're living in the city this winter?"

She turned her head to look at him. Her

dark eyes looked ever so serious, but she was smiling. "I'd like that."

"And will you write me in return?" he asked hopefully.

She nodded. "If I'm not kept too busy with my factory job."

"Do you know where you'll be working?"

"Not yet, but I'll be eighteen on January 5, and I'm gettin' stronger every year. I can probably get a job at most any of the factories. Even the ones where the work is heavy or dangerous."

Mike's heart clenched. "Please don't take a job that might put you in danger. I couldn't stand it if something were to happen to you, Kelly."

She gave him a questioning look.

"I love you, and I—" Mike never finished his sentence. Instead, he took Kelly in his arms and kissed her upturned mouth. Her lips tasted sweet as honey, and it felt so right to hold her.

When Kelly slipped her hands around his

neck and returned his kiss, Mike thought he was going to drown in the love he felt for her.

Kelly was the first to pull away. Her face was bright pink, and her eyes were cloudy with obvious emotion. Had she enjoyed the kiss as much as he?

She placed her trembling hands against her rosy cheeks. "I. . .I think it's time to go."

"But we haven't picked any wildflowers for you to use as watercolors," Mike argued.

She stood and dropped her art supplies into the pocket of her skirt. "I shouldn't have let you kiss me. It wasn't right."

Mike jumped to his feet. "It felt right to me."

She hung her head. "It wasn't, and it can never happen again."

Mike's previous elation plummeted clear to his toes. "I'm sorry you didn't enjoy the kiss."

"I did," she surprised him by saying. "But we can never be more than friends, and I don't think friends should go around kissin' each other."

So that's how it was. Kelly only saw him as

a friend. Mike felt like a fool. He'd read more into her physical response than there was. He'd decided awhile back to take it slow and easy with Kelly—be sure of her feelings before he made a move. He'd really messed things up, and it was too late to take back the kiss or his declaration of love.

"Forgive me for taking liberties that weren't mine," he said, forcing her to look him in the eye, even though it pained him to see there were tears running down her cheeks.

When she didn't say anything, Mike bent to retrieve the picnic basket and blanket. "I think you're right. It's time to go."

All the way back to the boat, Kelly chided herself for being foolish enough to allow Mike to kiss her. Now she'd hurt his feelings. It was obvious by the slump of his shoulders and the silence that covered the distance between them. On the way to the pond, he'd been talkative and whistled. Now the only sounds were the call of a dove and the canal waters lapping against the bank.

I was wrong to let him kiss me, but was I wrong to tell him we could only be friends? Should I have let him believe I might feel more for him than friendship? Do I feel more?

Kelly's disconcerting thoughts came to a halt when they rounded the bend where the canal boats could be seen. In the middle of the grassy area between Mike's store and the boats that had stopped for the day, two men were fistfighting. One was Patrick O'Malley. The other was Kelly's dad. Several other men stood on the sidelines, shouting, clapping, and cheering them on. What was the scuffle about, and why wasn't someone trying to stop it?

As though Mike could read her thoughts, he set the picnic basket and blanket on the ground, then stepped forward. "Please, no fighting on the Sabbath. Can't you two men solve your differences without the use of your knuckles?"

Pow! Papa's fist connected on the left side

of Patrick's chin. "You stay outa this, boy!" he shouted at Mike.

Smack! Patrick gave Papa a head butt that sent him sprawling on the grass.

"Stop it! Stop it!" Kelly shouted. Tears stung the backs of her eyes, and she felt herself tremble. Why must Papa make such a spectacle of himself? What did Mike and the others who were watching think of her dad?

The men were hitting each other lickety-split now, apparently oblivious to anything that was being said. Closer and closer to the canal they went, and when Papa slammed his fist into Patrick's chest, the man lost his footing and fell over backward. He grabbed Papa's shirtsleeve, and both men landed in the water with a splash.

Mortified, Kelly covered her face with her hands. How could a day that started out with such promise end on such a sour note?

After the fight was over and the two men settled down, Kelly learned the reason behind the scuffle. It had all started over something as simple as whose boat would be leaving first come Monday morning.

After the way her dad had caused such a scene, Kelly didn't think she could show her face to Mike or anyone else without suspecting they were talking behind her back. It was embarrassing the way her dad could fly off the handle and punch a man for no reason at all. Men didn't make a lick of sense!

CHAPTER 20

———❖———

As summer moved into fall, Kelly saw less of Mike. Papa kept them moving, wanting to make as many loads as possible before the bad weather. He refused to stop for anything that wasn't necessary.

It was just as well she wasn't spending time with Mike, Kelly decided as she sat upon Hector's back, bone tired and unable to take another step. After Mike's unexpected kiss the day they'd had a picnic by the Millers' pond,

Kelly hadn't wanted to do or say anything that might cause Mike to believe they had anything more than a casual friendship. What if Mike was thinking about marriage? What if he only felt sorry for her because she worked so hard? Kelly wasn't about to marry someone just to get away from Papa.

"I wish I didn't like Mike so much," Kelly murmured against the mule's ear.

It had been a long day, and Mike was about ready to close up his store when Betsy Nelson showed up. She seemed to have such good timing. Mike had just finished going through a stack of mail brought in by the last boat, and he was feeling lower than the canal waters after a break. He'd gotten another letter from his brother Alvin. This one said his other brother John had also found himself a girlfriend. There was even mention of a double wedding come December.

"Sorry to be coming by so late in the day,"

Kelly's Chance

Betsy panted, "but Papa's real sick, and I need some medicine to help quiet his cough." Her cheeks were red, and it was obvious by her heavy breathing that she'd probably run all the way to Mike's store. Mike knew Preacher Nelson didn't own a horse, preferring to make all his calls on foot.

"Come inside, and I'll see what kind of cough syrup I've got left in stock." Mike stepped aside so Betsy could enter, and she followed him to the back of the store.

"I haven't seen you for a while," Betsy said as Mike handed her a bottle of his best-selling cough syrup.

"I've been kinda busy."

Her eyelids fluttered. "I've missed you."

Mike swallowed hard. Betsy was flirting again, and it made him real nervous. He didn't want to hurt her feelings, but the simple fact was he didn't love Betsy. Even though Kelly had spurned his kiss, he was hoping someday she would come to love him as much as he did her.

241

As lonely as Mike was, and as much as he desired a wife, he knew he couldn't marry the preacher's daughter. She was too self-centered and a bit short-tempered, which probably meant she wouldn't be a patient mother. Kelly, on the other hand, would make a good wife and mother. It wasn't just her lovely face or long brown hair that had captured Mike's heart. Kelly had a gentle spirit. He'd witnessed it several times when she tended the mules. If only she seemed more willing.

Maybe I should quit praying for a wife and get a dog instead.

"Mike? Did you hear what I said?"

Betsy's high-pitched voice drove Mike's musings to the back of his mind. "What was that?"

"I said, 'I've missed you.' "

Mike felt his ears begin to warm. "Thank you, Betsy. It's nice to know I've been missed."

She looked at him with pleading eyes. No doubt she was hoping he would respond by saying he missed her, too. Mike couldn't lie. It wouldn't be right to lead Betsy on.

He moved quickly to the front of the store and placed the bottle of medicine on the counter. "Is there anything else you'll be needin'?"

Betsy's lower lip protruded as she shook her head.

He slipped the bottle into a brown paper sack, took her money, and handed Betsy her purchase. "I hope your dad is feeling better soon. Give him my regards, will you?"

She gave him a curt nod, lifted her head high, and pranced out the door. Mike let out a sigh of relief. At least she hadn't invited him to supper again.

The last day of November arrived, and Kelly couldn't believe it was time to leave the Lehigh Navigation System until spring. When Mama said she needed a few things, Papa had agreed to stop by Cooper's General Store. Kelly felt a mixture of relief and anxiety. Even though she wanted the chance to say good-bye, she dreaded seeing Mike again. Ever since the day he'd kissed her, things had been strained between them. She was afraid Mike wanted more from her than she was able to give. He'd said once that he wanted a whole passel of children so he could teach them responsibility. Did he think making children work would make them smart?

"I wonder if he wants kids so he can force 'em to labor with no pay," Kelly fumed to the mules. All the men she knew who put their kids to work paid them little or nothing. It wasn't fair! No wonder Sarah ran away and got married.

" 'Course if Sarah hadn't run off, I wouldn't have been left with all the work. Maybe the two of us could have come up with a plan to make money of our own."

They stopped in front of Mike's store, and Kelly secured the mules to a tree while she waited for her parents to get off the boat. A short time later, Mama disembarked.

"Where's Papa?" Kelly asked her mother.

Mama shrugged her shoulders. "He said he thought he'd take a nap while we do our shoppin'. He gave me a list of things he needs and said for us not to take all day."

Kelly followed her mother inside the store. She was glad to see Mike was busy with a customer. At least she wouldn't have to speak with him right away. It would give her time to think of something sensible to say. Should she ask if he still planned to write her while she was living in Easton? Should she promise to write him in return?

She thought about the paintings she had in her drawing tablet, which she hoped to give Mike before she left. Trouble was, she didn't want Mama to see. Could she find some way of speaking to Mike alone?

As if by divine intervention, the man Mike had been waiting on left the store, and about the same time, Mama decided to go back to the boat. She said something about needing to get Papa's opinion on the material she planned to use for a shirt she'd be making him soon.

Kelly knew she didn't have much time, so when the door closed behind her mother, she moved over to the counter where Mike stood.

"Hello, Kelly," he said, offering her a pleasant smile. "It's good to see you."

She moistened her lips with the tip of her tongue. "We're on our way to Easton for the winter and decided to stop by your store for a few items."

When Mike made no comment, Kelly rushed on before she lost her nerve. "I've got a few more paintings to give you. That is, if you're interested in tryin' to sell them." She reached into her pocket and withdrew the tablet, then placed it on the counter.

Mike thumbed through the pages. "These are great, Kelly. I especially like the one of the two children playing in a pile of fallen leaves."

Kelly smiled. That was her favorite picture, too. She'd drawn it in charcoal, then used a mixture of coffee shades, as well as some carrot, onion, and beet water for the colored leaves.

"I've sold a couple more pictures since you were last here," Mike said, reaching into his cash box and producing a few bills, which he handed to Kelly.

"What about your share of the profits?" she asked. "Did ya keep out some of the money?"

Mike gave her a sheepish grin. "I thought with you going to the big city and all, you'd probably need a little extra cash. I'll take my share out of the next batch of pictures I sell."

Kelly was tempted to argue, but the thought of having more money made her think twice about refusing. She nodded instead and slipped the bills into her pocket.

"When do you think you'll be back?" Mike asked.

"Sometime in March, whenever the ice and snow are gone."

"Is there an address where I can write to you?"

"We'll be staying at Mable Flannigan's Boardinghouse. It's on the corner of Front Street in the eight hundred block."

"And you can write me here at Cooper's General Store, Walnutport, Pennsylvania."

"I'll try to write if there's time." That was all Kelly could promise. She had no idea where she might be working or how many hours she'd be putting in each day.

"Mind if I give you a hug good-bye?" Mike asked. "Just as friends?"

Kelly wasn't sure what to say. She didn't want to encourage Mike, yet she didn't want to be rude, either. She guessed one little hug wouldn't hurt. He did say it was just as friends. She nodded and held out her arms.

Mike skirted around the counter and pulled her into an embrace.

Kelly's heart pounded against her chest, and she feared it might burst wide open. What if Mama came back and saw the two of them? What if Mike decided to kiss her again?

Her fears were relieved when Mike pulled away. "Take care, Kelly McGregor. I'll see you next spring."

CHAPTER 21

Winter came quickly to the Lehigh Valley, and a thick layer of snow soon covered the ground. Mike missed Kelly terribly, and several times a week he walked the towpath, as he was now, thinking about her and praying for her safety. He knew she cared for him, but only as a friend. If he just hadn't allowed himself to fall in love with her. If only she loved him in return.

Kelly had been gone a little over a month,

and still not one letter had he received. He'd written to her several times, but no response. Was she too busy to write? Had she found a man and fallen in love? All sorts of possible explanations flitted through Mike's mind as he trudged along, his boots crunching through the fresh-fallen snow.

God would need to heal his heart if Kelly never returned, because Mike was in love with her, and there didn't seem to be a thing he could do about it.

I shouldn't have let myself fall for her, Lord, he prayed. *What I thought was Your will might have only been my own selfish desires. Maybe You want me to remain single.*

Shivering against the cold, Mike headed back to his house. There was no point in going over this again and again. If Kelly came back to the canal in the spring with a different attitude toward him, Mike would be glad. If she didn't, then he would have to accept it as God's will.

When Mike stepped inside the house a short time later, a blast of warm air hit him in the face. It was a welcome relief from the cold. As he hung his coat on a wall peg, he noticed the calendar hanging nearby. Today was January 5, Kelly's eighteenth birthday. He remembered her mentioning it before she left for the city. He'd sent her a package several days ago and hoped she would receive it on time. Even more than that, Mike hoped she liked the birthday present he'd chosen.

Kelly couldn't believe how bad her feet hurt. She was used to walking the towpath every day, but trudging through the hilly city of Easton was an entirely different matter. Papa had insisted Kelly get a job to help with expenses, and she'd been out looking almost every day since they had arrived at the boardinghouse in Easton. No one seemed to be hiring right before Christmas, and after the holidays, she was told either that there was no work or that she wasn't qualified for any of the available positions. Kelly kept looking, and in the evenings and on weekends, she helped Mama sew and clean their small, three-room flat.

Kelly hated to spend her days looking for work and longed to be with their mules that had been left at Morgan's Stables just outside of town. It wasn't cheap to keep them there, but Papa said they had no choice. Needing money for the mules' care was one of the reasons he'd taken a job at Glendon Iron Furnace, which overlooked the canal and Lehigh Valley Railroad. The work was hard and heavy, but pay was better than at many other manual jobs.

Every chance she got, Kelly went to see her animal friends. Today was her eighteenth birthday, and she'd decided to celebrate with a trip to the stables right after breakfast. It might be the only thing special about her birthday, since neither Mama nor Papa had made any mention of it. They'd been sitting around the breakfast table for ten minutes, and no one had said a word about what day it was. Papa had his nose in the *Sunday Call*, Easton's newspaper, and Mama seemed preoccupied with the scrambled eggs on her plate.

Kelly sighed deeply and drank some tea. It didn't matter. She'd never had much of a fuss made on her birthday anyway. Why should this year be any different?

Maybe I'll take some of the money I earned sellin' paintings and buy something today. Kelly grimaced. She knew she should save all her cash for that art gallery she hoped to open some day. Even as the idea popped into her mind, Kelly felt it was futile. She'd only sold a few paintings so far, and even if she sold more, it would take years before she'd have enough to open any kind of gallery. She would need to pay rent for a building, and then there was the cost of all the supplies. It wouldn't be enough to simply sell her paintings and drawings; she'd want to offer her customers the chance to purchase paper, paints, charcoal pencils, and maybe some fancy frames. All that would cost a lot of money. Money Kelly would probably never see in her lifetime.

I may as well give up my dream. If I can find a job in the city, it would probably be best if I stay here and work. Papa can hire a mule driver to take my place. It would serve him right if I never went back to the canal.

A loud knock drove Kelly's thoughts to the back of her mind. She looked at Papa, then Mama. Neither one seemed interested in answering the door.

Kelly sighed and pushed her chair away from the table. Why was she always expected to do everything? She shuffled across the room, feeling as though she had the weight of the world on her shoulders.

She opened the door and was greeted by their landlord, Mable Flannigan. A heavyset, middle-aged woman with bright red hair and sparking blue eyes, Mable had told them that her husband was killed in the War Between the States, and she'd been on her own ever since. The woman had no children to care for and had opened her home to boarders shortly after the war ended nearly twenty-seven years ago. Kelly always wondered why Mrs. Flannigan had never remarried. Could be that she was still pining for her dead husband, or maybe the woman thought she could get along better without a man.

"This came for you in the mornin's mail," Mrs. Flannigan said, holding out a package wrapped in brown paper.

Kelly's forehead wrinkled. "For me?" She couldn't imagine who would be sending her anything.

The older woman nodded. "It has your name and the address of my boardinghouse right here on the front."

Kelly took the package and studied the handwriting. Her name was there all right, in big, bold letters. Her heart began to pound, and her hands shook when she saw the return address. It was from Mike Cooper.

Remembering her manners, Kelly opened the door wider. "Would ya like to come in and have a cup of coffee or some tea?"

Mrs. Flannigan shook her head. "Thanks,

but I'd better not. I've got me some washin' to do today, and it sure won't get done if I lollygag over a cup of hot coffee."

The woman turned to go, and Kelly called, "Thanks for deliverin' the package."

A few seconds later, Kelly sat on the sofa, tearing the brown paper away from the box. With trembling hands, she lifted the lid. She let out a little gasp when she saw what the box contained. Her eyes feasted on a tin of store-bought watercolor paints, a real artist's tablet, and three brushes in various sizes. There was also a note:

Dear Kelly,

I wanted you to have this paint set for your eighteenth birthday. I only wish I could be with you to help celebrate. I hope you're doing all right, and I'm real anxious for you to return to the canal.

Fondly, your friend,
Mike Cooper

P.S. Please write soon.

Kelly's Chance

Kelly sat for several seconds, trying to understand how Mike could have known today was her birthday and relishing the joy of owning a real set of watercolors, not to mention a store-bought tablet that she hadn't put together herself. She would be able to paint anything she wanted now, using nearly every shade imaginable.

An image of Mike's friendly face flashed into Kelly's mind. She might have mentioned something to him about her birthday being on January 5. The fact that he'd remembered and cared enough to send her a present was almost overwhelming. No one had ever given her a gift like the one she held in her hands.

"Kelly, who was at the door?" Papa hollered from the next room.

She swallowed hard and stood up. Her dad might be mad when he saw the present Mike had sent her, but she wouldn't lie or hide it from him. While Papa was at work, and after Kelly got home from searching for a job every day, Mama had been reading the Bible out loud, and Kelly had fallen under deep conviction. She'd strayed from God and knew she needed to make things right. It was wrong to lie or hide the truth from her parents. It had been a sin to harbor resentment toward Papa, and with the Lord's help, she was doing much better in that regard.

Grasping the box with her birthday present inside, Kelly walked back to the kitchen. "Mrs. Flannigan was at the door with a package for me." Kelly placed the box on the table.

"Who would be sendin' you anything?" Papa asked, his eyebrows drawing together.

"It's from Mike Cooper."

"The storekeeper along the canal?" Mama questioned as she peered into the box.

Kelly nodded. "It's for my birthday." She sank into her chair, wondering when the explosion would come.

Mama pulled the tin of watercolors out of the box and held it up. Papa frowned but didn't say a word. Kelly held her breath.

"What a thoughtful gift," Mama said.

"Now you'll be able to paint with real colors instead of makin' colored water out of my vegetables."

Kelly felt her face heat up. So her mother had known all the time that she was taking carrots, beets, and onions out of the bin. Funny thing, Mama had never said a word about it until now.

"Humph!" Papa snorted. "I hope that man don't think his gift is gonna buy him my daughter's hand in marriage."

"Mike and I are just friends, Papa," Kelly was quick to say. She turned to face him. "Can I keep it? I promise not to paint when I'm supposed to be workin'."

"You've gotta find a job first," Papa grumbled. "We've been in the city for a whole month already, and not one red cent have you brought in."

"I'll look again on Monday," Kelly promised.

"Why don'tcha try over at the Simon Silk Mill on Bushkill Creek?" Mama suggested. "I hear tell they're lookin' to hire a few people there."

Kelly nodded. "I'll go first thing on Monday."

Papa took a long drink from his cup of coffee, wiped his mouth with the back of his hand, and stood up. "I need to get to work."

"But it's Saturday," Mama reminded.

He leveled her with a disgruntled look. "Don'tcha think I know that, woman? They're operatin' the plant six days a week now, and I volunteered to come in today." His gaze swung over to Kelly. "You can keep the birthday present, but I'd better not find you paintin' when ya should be out lookin' for work."

"Thank you, Papa, and I promise I won't paint until all my chores are done for the day, neither." Kelly felt like she could kiss her dad. She didn't, though. Papa had never been very affectionate, and truth be told, until this moment, Kelly had never felt like kissing him.

Papa grunted, grabbed his jacket off the wall peg, and sauntered out the door.

Mama patted Kelly's hand. "Tonight I'm fixin' your favorite supper in honor of your birthday."

"Hunks-a-go pudding and roast beef?" Kelly asked hopefully.

Mama nodded and grinned. "Might make a chocolate cake for dessert, too."

Kelly smiled in return, feeling better than she had in weeks. Today turned out to be a better birthday than she'd ever imagined. Now if she could only find a job.

CHAPTER 22

———————❖———————

As Kelly stood in front of the brick building that housed the Simon Silk Mill, she whispered a prayer, petitioning God to give her a job. She didn't know any other kind of work besides leading the mules, but Mama had taught her to sew, and she figured that's what she would be doing if she were hired here. All the other times they'd wintered in Easton, Papa had never demanded Kelly find a job. That was probably because Mama insisted Kelly go to school. She was older now and done with book learning, so it was time to make some money. If only she didn't have to give it all to Papa. If she could keep the money she earned, Kelly would probably have enough to open her art gallery in no time at all. Of course, she didn't think she would have the nerve to tell Papa she wasn't going back to the canal in the spring.

Pushing the door open, Kelly stepped inside the factory and located the main office. She entered the room and told the receptionist she needed a job. Disappointment flooded Kelly's soul when she was told all the positions at the mill had been taken.

Kelly left the office feeling a sense of frustration. What if she never found a job? Papa would be furious and might make her throw out her art supplies. She couldn't let that happen. There had to be something she could do.

Kelly was almost to the front door when she bumped into someone. Her mouth dropped open, and she took a step back. "Sarah?"

Wanda E. Brunstetter

The young woman with dark brown hair piled high on her head looked at Kelly as if she'd seen a ghost. "Kelly, is that you?"

"It's me, Sarah. I'm so surprised to see you."

"And I, you," her sister replied.

"Do you work here?"

Sarah nodded. "Have been for the last couple of months. Before that, I was home takin' care of little Sam."

"Little Sam?"

"Sam Jr."

"You have a son?" Kelly could hardly believe her sister had a baby they knew nothing about. For that matter, they hadn't heard anything from Sarah since that one letter telling the family she and Sam had gotten married and were living in New Jersey.

"The baby was born six months ago," Sarah explained. "Sam was workin' at Warren Soapstone, but one day he lost his temper with the boss and got fired. So I had to find work, and he's been home takin' care of the baby ever since."

Kelly stood, studying her sister and trying to let all she'd said sink in. Sarah was dressed in a beige-colored cotton blouse and plain brown skirt covered with a black apron. Her shoulders were slumped, and she looked awful tired.

The fact that Sam Turner would allow his wife to work while he stayed home was one more proof for Kelly that men only used women. Sam was no better than Papa. Sarah had run off with Sam to get away from working, and now she was being forced to support not only herself, but her husband and baby as well. It made Kelly sick to the pit of her stomach.

"Are you and the folks stayin' at the boardinghouse like before?" Sarah's question drove Kelly's thoughts to the back of her mind.

"Yes, we've been there since early December." Kelly gave her sister a hug. "I'm sure Mama and Papa would like to see you and the baby. . .Sam Sr., too."

When Sarah pulled away, tears stood in

her dark eyes. "Oh, please don't say anything to the folks about seein' me today."

"Why not?"

"Papa always hated Sam, and when we tried to tell him we were in love and wanted to get married, he blew up and said if we did, he'd punch Sam in the nose."

Kelly flinched at the memory. She'd been there and could understand why her sister might be afraid to confront their dad now.

"I won't say a word," Kelly promised, "but I would sure like to see my nephew. You think there's any way that could be arranged?"

Sarah gave a tired smile. "I'd like you to meet little Sam. Mama, too, for that matter. Maybe the two of you can come by our apartment sometime soon. Let me talk it over with my husband first, though."

"How will we get in touch with you?"

Sarah looked thoughtful. "Is Papa workin' every day?"

Kelly nodded. "Over at Glendon Iron Furnace, even Saturdays now."

"Then how about if the baby and I come by the boardinghouse next Saturday?"

"That would be great. Should I tell Mama ahead, or do you want to surprise her?"

"Let's make it our little surprise." Sarah squeezed Kelly's arm. "I need to get back up to the second floor where I work on one of the weavin' looms."

Kelly gave her sister another hug. "Sure is good to see you, Sarah."

"Same here." Sarah started for the stairs, and Kelly headed for the front door, feeling more cheerful than she had all morning. Even if she didn't have a job, at least she'd been reunited with her sister. That was something to be grateful for.

For the third time that morning, Mike sorted through the stack of mail he'd dumped on the counter after it arrived by canal boat. There was nothing from Kelly. Wasn't she ever going to respond? Had she received his birthday present? Did she like the watercolor set, sketching pad, and paintbrushes, or was she mad at him for giving them to her? If only she'd written a note to let him know the package had arrived.

"I've got to get busy and quit thinking about Kelly." Mike slipped each letter into the cubbyholes he'd made for his postal customers. The packages were kept in a box underneath. As local people dropped by the store, he would hand out their mail and be glad he'd taken the time to organize it so well. Any mail that came for the boatmen who were working in the city and wanted their parcels to be held until they returned to the canal was stored safely in a wooden box under the front counter. Most canalers lived in homes nearby, and those, like Amos McGregor, would be getting their mail forwarded to their temporary address during the winter months.

Thinking about Amos caused Mike's mind to wander back to Kelly. Whenever he closed his eyes at night, he could see her smiling face, hear her joyous laughter, and feel her sweet lips against his own. Had it been wrong to kiss her? He hadn't thought so at the time, but after she'd pulled away and cooled off toward him, Mike figured he'd done a terrible thing.

"I kept telling myself I would go slow with Kelly, but I moved too fast." Mike moaned. "Why must I always rush ahead of God?" He reached for one of the Bibles he had stacked near the end of the counter and opened it to the book of Hebrews. He found chapter 10 and read verses 35 and 36: *"Cast not away. . .your confidence, which hath great recompense of reward. For ye have need of patience, that, after ye have done the will of God, ye might receive the promise."*

Mike closed his eyes and quoted Genesis 2:18: " 'And the Lord God said, It is not good that the man should be alone; I will make him an help meet for him.' " He dropped to his knees behind the counter. "Oh, Lord, if I have patience and continue to do Your will, might I receive the promise of an help meet?"

Except for the eerie howling of the wind

against the eaves of the store, there was no sound. Patience. Mike knew he needed to be more patient. With God's help he would try, but it wouldn't be easy.

CHAPTER 23

———❖———

On Saturday afternoon, Sarah, with baby Sam tucked under one arm, came by the boardinghouse. Kelly was shocked at her sister's haggard appearance. Sarah had looked tired the other day, but it was nothing like this. Puffiness surrounded her sister's red-rimmed eyes, indicating she had been crying. Something was wrong. Kelly could feel it in her bones.

Mama, who hadn't been told about Sarah's surprise visit, rushed to her oldest daughter's side when Kelly stepped away and closed the door. "Sarah!" Mama exclaimed. "I can't believe it's you. Where have you been livin'? How did you know we'd be here?" She reached out to touch the baby's chubby hand. "And who is this cute little fellow?"

Sarah emitted a small laugh, even though her expression was strained. "Too many questions at once, Mama. Can I come in and be seated before I answer each one?"

Mama's hands went to her flushed cheeks. "Yes, yes. Please, let me have your coats, then go into the livin' room and get comfortable."

Sarah turned to Kelly, who so far hadn't uttered a word. "Would ya mind holdin' Sam while I take off my coat?"

Kelly held out her arms to the child, but little Sam buried his head against his mother's chest and whimpered.

"He's a bit shy around strangers," Sarah said. "I'm sure he'll warm up to you soon." She handed the baby over to Kelly despite the child's protests.

Feeling awkward and unsure of herself, Kelly stepped into the living room and took a seat on the sofa. Baby Sam squirmed restlessly, but he didn't cry.

A few minutes later, Sarah and their mother entered the room. Mama sat beside Kelly on the sofa, and Sarah took a seat in the rocking chair across from them.

"Mama, meet your grandson, Sam Jr.," Sarah announced.

Mama's lips curved into a smile, and she reached out to take the infant from Kelly. He went willingly, obviously drawn to his grandma.

"I can't believe you have a baby, Sarah. How old is he, and why didn't ya write and tell us about him?"

Sarah hung her head, and Kelly noticed tears dripping onto her sister's skirt, leaving dark spots in the gray-colored fabric. "I—I knew you and Papa were angry with me for runnin' off with Sam, so I figured you wouldn't want to know anything about what I was doin'."

Kelly closed her eyes and offered up a prayer on her sister's behalf as she waited for her mother's reply.

Mama's eyes filled with tears, and she hugged the baby to her chest. "I could never turn my back on one of my own, Sarah. I love both my girls." She glanced over at Kelly, who was also close to tears.

"I love you, too, Mama," Kelly murmured.

"So do I," Sarah agreed. "Now as to your questions, Sam is six months old, and we've all been livin' in a flat across the bridge in Phillipsburg. Up until a few weeks ago, Sam worked at Warren Soapstone, but he got fired for shootin' off his mouth to the boss." Sarah paused and drew in a deep breath. "I've been workin' at the Simon Silk Mill ever since, and Sam *was* takin' care of the baby."

Was? What did Sarah mean by that? Before Kelly could voice the question, her sister rushed on.

"Sam's been drinkin' here of late, and actin' real funny. Last night when I got home

274

from work, he had his bags packed and said he was leavin' me and the baby." Sarah's eyes clouded with fresh tears, and she choked on a sob. "I've got no place to leave Sam Jr. while I'm at work now, and I can't afford to hire a babysitter and pay the rent on my flat, too."

"I could watch the baby for you," Kelly spoke up. "I haven't been able to find work anywhere yet, so I have nothin' else to do with my time." *Except paint and dream impossible dreams*, she added mentally.

Sarah shot Mama an imploring look. "Would ya allow Kelly to come live with me?"

"I'm not sure that would set well with your papa." Mama pursed her lips. "Why don't you and the baby move in here with us?"

Sarah glanced around the room. "This is the same place you've always rented from Mable Flannigan, right?"

Their mother nodded.

"Mama, it's so small. There's not nearly enough room for two extra people." She nodded at Kelly. "If you could come stay with me and Sam Jr., I couldn't pay you, but I could offer free room and board. You'd also have a small room, which you'd need to share with the baby."

As sorry as Kelly was to hear the news that Sarah's husband had left, the idea of moving in with her sister sounded rather pleasant. It would give her more time to paint without Papa breathing down her neck or hollering because she still hadn't found a job. She touched her mother's arm gently. "Please, Mama. I'd like to help Sarah out in her time of need."

Mama shrugged. "If Papa says it's all right, then I'll agree to it as well."

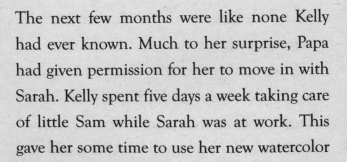

The next few months were like none Kelly had ever known. Much to her surprise, Papa had given permission for her to move in with Sarah. Kelly spent five days a week taking care of little Sam while Sarah was at work. This gave her some time to use her new watercolor set, since she could paint or draw whenever the baby slept.

Besides babysitting, Kelly cleaned the apartment, did most of the cooking, and even sewed new clothes for her fast-growing nephew. She and little Sam had become good friends, and Kelly discovered she was more capable with children than she'd ever imagined.

As Kelly sat in the rocking chair, trying to get the baby to sleep, she let her mind wander back to the general store outside of Walnutport. A vision of Mike Cooper flashed across her mind. He was good with children. Kelly had witnessed him giving out free candy to several of the kids who played along the canal and to many who visited his store, as well. Mike wanted a whole houseful of children; he'd told her so.

"I never did write and thank Mike for the birthday gift," Kelly whispered against little Sam's downy blond head. The baby looked a lot like his papa, but Kelly hoped he didn't grow up to be anything like the man. How could Sam Turner have left his wife and child? Just thinking about it made Kelly's blood boil. Was Mike Cooper any different from Papa or Sam? Could he be trusted not to hurt her the way Papa often did or the way Sam had done to Sarah?

Mike had promised to write, and he'd done so several times. He'd also sent her a wonderful present. He might not be the same as other men she knew. Kelly guessed she'd have to make up her mind about Mike when they returned to the canal sometime in March.

She bent her head and kissed the tip of little Sam's nose. "You and your mama might be goin' with us this spring. I don't rightly see how the two of you can stay on here by yourselves." She giggled at the baby's response to her kiss. He'd scrunched up his nose and wiggled his lips, almost as if he was trying to kiss her back.

"Of course, I could always stay on here, I suppose. Papa can't make me return to the canal if I don't want to." Even as the words slipped off her tongue, Kelly knew what she would do when Papa said it was time to return to their boat. She would go along willingly because she missed her mule friends, missed the smell of fresh air, and yes, even missed Mike Cooper.

❊

Mike stared at his empty coffee cup. He should clear away the breakfast dishes and get his horse hitched to the buckboard. He was expecting a load of supplies to be delivered to Walnutport today by train, and it would be good if he were there when it came in. Mike knew that Gus Stevens, who ran the livery stable next to the train station, would be happy to take the supplies to his place and hold them for him, but Mike didn't like to take advantage of the older man's good nature.

With that thought in mind, Mike scooped the dishes off the table and set them in the sink. He'd pour warm water over them and let them soak until he returned from town.

A short time later, Mike climbed into his wagon, clucked to the horse, and headed toward Walnutport. During the first part of the trip, he sang favorite hymns and played his mouth harp. It made the time go quicker and caused Mike to feel a bit closer to his Maker. It also made him feel less lonely.

As the days had turned into weeks, and the weeks into months, Mike's yearning for a wife had not diminished. He'd been feeling so lonely here of late, he'd actually considered accepting one of Betsy Nelson's frequent supper invitations. The woman was persistent, he'd give her that much. Persistent and pushy. Nothing like Kelly McGregor.

"I've got to quit thinking about Kelly," Mike berated himself. "She obviously feels nothing for me. If she did, she would have written by now." Mike wasn't sure he'd ever see Kelly again. For all he knew, she'd decided to stay in the city of Easton. She'd probably found a job and a boyfriend. She could even be married.

By the time Mike arrived at his destination, he was sweating worse than his horse. He'd let the gelding run and had enjoyed the exhilarating ride. It helped clear his thinking. Nothing else had mattered but the wind blowing against his face. Tomorrow would be a new day. Another time to reflect on God's will for Mike's life.

CHAPTER 24

On Monday morning, the third week of March, the McGregors boarded their boat. The canal was full of water again, and Papa was most anxious to get started hauling coal. Sarah and baby Sam had come along, since Sarah didn't want to stay in Easton by herself and couldn't talk Kelly into staying on. Besides, Mama could use Sarah's help on the boat and would be available to watch the baby whenever Kelly's sister took over walking the mules.

Kelly felt bad that Sarah was returning to the canal she'd hated so much, but it would be nice to have her sister's help, as well as her companionship.

Kelly looked forward to stopping by Cooper's General Store Tuesday afternoon. While they'd picked up some supplies at Dull's Grocery Store in Easton, Papa had forgotten a couple of things and was planning on getting them at Mike's store. Kelly planned to give Mike several more pictures to try to sell, as she'd been able to paint many during her stay in the city. She was also anxious to see whether he'd sold any of her other pieces. She hoped she could continue their business relationship without Mike expecting anything more.

Kelly pulled the collar of her jacket tightly against her chin as she tromped along the towpath, singing her favorite song and not even minding the chilly March winds.

"Hunks-a-go pudding and pieces of pie; my mother gave me when I was knee-high. . . . And if you don't believe it, just drop in and see—the hunks-a-go pudding my mother gave me."

Mike felt better than he had in weeks. He'd had several customers and given away a couple of Bibles to some rough-and-tumble canalers who were desperately in need of God. Mike had witnessed these two men fighting on more than one occasion, and the fact that they'd willingly taken a Bible gave him hope that others might also be receptive to the Gospel.

As Mike washed the store windows with a rag and some diluted ammonia, he thought about Kelly's dad. Now there was a man badly in need of the Lord. Mike had witnessed Amos McGregor's temper several times. If Amos found forgiveness for his sins and turned his life around, maybe Kelly would be more receptive to Mike's attentions. He was sure the main reason Kelly was so standoffish was because she was afraid of men.

He glanced at the wall behind his front

counter. Only two of Kelly's pictures had sold since she'd left for Easton, and those had both been bought before Christmas. No one had shown any interest in her work since then, even though Mike often pointed the pictures out to his customers, hoping they would take the hint and buy one.

Mike studied the window he'd been washing, checking for any spots or streaks. To his surprise, Amos McGregor's boat was docked out front, and the man was heading toward the store. Trudging alongside of Amos was his wife, Dorrie, Kelly, and another woman carrying a young child.

Mike climbed off his ladder and hurried to the front of the store. Kelly had returned to the canal! He opened the door and greeted his customers with a smile and a sense of excitement. "It's sure nice to see you folks again."

Amos grunted in reply, but Kelly returned his smile. "It's good to be back," she said.

"And who might this little guy be?" Mike asked, reaching out to clasp the chubby fingers

285

of the little boy who was held by the other young woman.

"That's baby Sam," Kelly said. "In case you don't remember, this is my sister, Sarah. She and Sam Jr. are gonna be livin' with us for a while."

"Yes, I remember Sarah." Mike nodded and smiled at Kelly's sister. He didn't ask for details. From the pathetic look on Sarah's face, he figured her marriage to Sam Turner was probably over.

"Do you have any soft material I might use for diapers?" Sarah asked. "Sam seems to go through them pretty fast, and I don't have time to be washin' every day."

Mike pointed to the shelf where he kept bolts of material. "I'm sure you'll find something to your liking over there."

Sarah moved away, and her mother followed. Amos was across the room looking at some new shovels Mike had recently gotten in, so apparently Kelly felt free to stare up at her paintings.

Mike positioned himself so he was standing beside Kelly. "How have you been? I've missed you," he whispered.

Her gaze darted from her dad, to the paintings, and back to Mike. "I'm fine, and I've brought you more pictures." She frowned. "But from the looks of it, you still have quite a few of my old ones."

He nodded. "Sorry to say I only sold two while you were gone." He leaned his head close to her ear. "Did you get the birthday present I sent? I'd hoped you would write and let me know."

"Yes, I got the package and put it to good use." Kelly averted his gaze. "Sorry for not writing to say thank you. I kept meaning to write, but I got busy takin' care of little Sam while Sarah went to work each day."

"That's okay. I understand." Mike touched her arm briefly, but then he pulled his hand away. "Do you have the new pictures with you now?"

She nodded, reached into her pocket,

retrieved the drawing tablet he'd sent her, and handed it to him. "I was able to make things look more real usin' things you sent me."

Mike thumbed quickly through the tablet. Pictures of row housing, tall buildings, and statues in the city of Easton covered the first pages. There were also some paintings of the bridge that spanned the river between Easton, Pennsylvania, and Phillipsburg, New Jersey, as well as a few pictures of people. They were all done well, and Mike was glad he'd sent Kelly the paint set, even if she hadn't chosen to write and tell him she'd received it. He was even happier that she'd accepted the gift and put it to good use.

"These are wonderful," he said. "Would you mind leaving them with me to try and sell?"

Kelly's eyebrows furrowed. "But you still have most of my other pictures. Why would ya be wantin' more?"

"Because they're good—really good," he asserted. "I've always admired your artwork, and I believe you've actually gotten better."

Her expression turned hopeful. "You really think so?"

"I do."

She pointed to the tablet. "And you think you can sell these?"

"I'd like to try."

She nodded her consent. "Do as you like then."

"Will you be spending the night in the area?" Mike asked.

Kelly opened her mouth, but her dad spoke up before she could say anything. "We'll be headin' on up the canal. Won't be back this way 'til probably late Saturday."

Mike turned his head to the left. He hadn't realized Kelly's dad was standing beside him, holding a shovel in one hand.

"You think you might stay over on Saturday night?"

"Could be," Amos said.

Mike smiled to himself. If the McGregors were here on Sunday, then he might get the chance to spend some time alone with Kelly. Even though the weather was still a bit chilly, it was possible that they'd be able to go on another picnic.

Kelly left Mike's store with mixed feelings. It was wonderful to see him again, but her spirits had been dampened when he'd told her he'd only sold two pictures during her absence. Mike had given her the money for those paintings as she was on her way out the door. He'd also whispered that he wanted to take her on another picnic and hoped it would be this Sunday, if they were near his store.

"Mind if I walk with you a ways?" Sarah asked, breaking into Kelly's musings. "Sam's ready for a nap, and Mama doesn't need me for anything. I thought the fresh air and exercise might do me some good."

Kelly was always glad for her sister's company. "You wanna be in charge of the mules or just offer me companionship?"

Kelly's Chance

"You can tend the mules," Sarah was quick to say. "I think they like you better than they do me."

"They're just used to me, that's all." Kelly adjusted the brim of her straw hat, which seemed to have a mind of its own. "Truth be told, I think old Herman kinda likes it when I sing silly canal songs."

"You sing to the mules?"

Kelly nodded. "Guess it's really for me, but if they enjoy it, then that makes it all the better."

Sarah chuckled. It was good to see her smile. She'd been so sad since her husband had run off, and Kelly couldn't blame her. She would be melancholy, too, if the man she'd married had chosen not to stay around and help out. Sam Turner ought to be tarred and feathered for walking out on his wife and baby. He probably never loved Sarah in the first place. Most likely he only married her just to show her folks that he could take their daughter away.

"Tell me about Mike Cooper," Sarah said.

Kelly jerked her head. "What about him?"

"Have you and him been courtin'?"

"What would make you ask that?"

Sarah gave Kelly a nudge in the ribs with her bony elbow. "He couldn't take his eyes off you the whole time we were in the store." She eyed Kelly curiously. "I'd say it's as plain as the nose on your face that you're smitten with him as well."

What could Kelly say in response? She couldn't deny her feelings for Mike. She enjoyed his company, and he was the best-looking man she'd ever laid eyes on. That didn't mean they were courting, though. And it sure didn't mean she was smitten with him.

"Mike and me have gone on a few picnics, but we're not a courtin' couple," Kelly said, shrugging her shoulders.

"But you'd like to be, right?" her sister prodded.

"We're just friends; nothin' more."

Sarah wiggled her dark eyebrows, then winked. "Whatever you say, little sister. Whatever you say."

CHAPTER 25

※

Early Saturday afternoon, Mike went outside to help one of the local boatmen load the supplies he had purchased onto his boat. They had no more than placed the last one on deck when Mike saw the McGregors' boat heading their way.

His heart did a little flip-flop. Would they be stopping for the night? Mike stepped onto the towpath, anxious for Kelly to arrive. While he waited, he slicked back his hair, finger-combed his mustache, and made sure his flannel shirt was tucked inside his trousers.

A few minutes later, Kelly and her mules were alongside him. The animals brayed and snorted, as if they expected him to give them a handout, as he'd done a few times before.

"Sorry, fellows, but I didn't know you were coming, so there aren't any apples or carrots in my pockets today." Mike gave each mule a pat on its flank, then he turned and smiled at Kelly. "I'm glad you're here. Are you planning to stay overnight?"

She shook her head. "Now that Sarah's here to help, Papa has us movin' twice as fast as before. He says there's no time to waste. Especially when we never know if there's gonna be trouble ahead that might slow us down."

Mike felt his anticipation slip to the toes of his boots. He'd been waiting so long to be with Kelly again, and now they weren't stopping? How was he ever going to tell her what was on his mind if they couldn't spend any time together?

"I'm sorry to hear you're not staying over," he muttered. "I was really hoping we'd be able to go on a picnic tomorrow afternoon."

"Isn't it a mite chilly for a picnic?"

Mike shrugged his shoulders. "I figured we could build a fire and snuggle beneath a blanket if it got too cold."

When Kelly smiled at him, he wanted to take her into his arms and proclaim his intentions. He knew now wasn't the time or the place, so he drew on his inner strength and took a step back. "When do you think you might be stopping long enough so we can spend a few minutes together?"

She turned her palms upward. "Don't know. That's entirely up to Papa."

Mike groaned. "Guess I'll just have to wait and ask God to give me more patience."

"Get a move on, would ya, girl?"

Kelly and Mike both turned. Amos McGregor was leaning over the side of the boat, and he wasn't smiling.

"I need to get the mules movin' again," Kelly said to Mike.

He stepped aside but touched her arm as she passed by. "See you soon, Kelly."

"I hope so," she murmured.

The next few weeks sped by, as Kelly and Sarah took turns leading the mules, and Papa kept the boat moving as fast as the animals would pull. They stopped only once for supplies, and that was at a store in Mauch Chunk. Kelly was beginning to think she'd never get the chance to see Mike Cooper again or find out if any of her paintings had sold. On days like today, when the sky was cloudy and threatened rain, Kelly's spirits plummeted, and she didn't feel much like praying. All the while they'd been living in Easton, she'd felt closer to God, reading her Bible every day and offering prayers on behalf of her family and her future. It didn't seem as if any of her prayers were going to be answered, and she wondered if she should continue to ask God for things He probably wouldn't provide.

She'd prayed for her sister, and look how that had turned out. She had prayed for Papa's salvation, yet he was still as moody and cantankerous as ever. She'd asked God to allow her to make enough money to support herself and open an art gallery, but that wasn't working out, either. So far, she'd only made a few dollars, which was a long ways from what she would need. It was an impossible dream, and with each passing day, Kelly became more convinced it was never going to happen.

She looked up at the darkening sky and prayed, "Lord, if walkin' the mules is the only job You have in mind for me, then help me learn to be content."

It was the end of April before Kelly saw Mike again. They'd arrived in front of his store at dusk on Saturday evening, so Papa decided to stay for the night. Since the next day was Sunday and the boatmen were not allowed to pull their loads up the canal, they would be around for the whole day.

Kelly settled into her bed, filled with a sense of joy she hadn't felt in weeks. Tomorrow she planned to attend the church service on the grassy area in front of Mike's store. Afterward she hoped to see Mike and talk to him about her artwork. She'd managed to do a few more paintings—mostly of little Sam—so she would give those to Mike as well.

Sam was growing so much, and soon he'd be toddling all over the place. Then they would have to be sure he was tied securely to something, or else he might end up falling overboard. Canal life could be dangerous, and precautions had to be taken in order to protect everyone on board. Even the mules needed safeguarding from bad weather, insects, freak accidents, and fatigue.

Kelly closed her eyes and drew in a deep breath as she snuggled into her feather pillow.

She fell asleep dreaming about Mike Cooper.

———❖———

Sunday morning brought sunshine and blue skies. It was perfect spring weather, and Kelly had invited her sister and mother to join her for the church service that had just begun. Mama said she'd better stay on the boat with Papa, but Sarah left the baby behind with her parents and joined Kelly.

The two young women spread a blanket on the grass and took a seat just as Betsy Nelson began playing her zither, while her father led those who had gathered in singing "Holy Spirit, Light Divine."

Kelly lifted her voice with the others. The first verse spoke to her heart:

Holy Spirit, Light divine,
    Shine upon this heart of mine.
Chase the shades of night away;
    Turn my darkness into day.

The song gave Kelly exactly what she needed. A reminder that only God could turn her darkness into day. As difficult as it was, she needed to keep praying and trusting Him to answer her prayers.

Kelly felt her sister's nudge in the ribs. "Psst. . . look who's watchin' you."

Kelly glanced around and noticed Mike sitting on a wooden box several feet away. He grinned and nodded at her, and she smiled in return.

"I told you he likes you."

Kelly put her fingers to her lips. "Shh. . . someone might hear."

Sarah snickered, but she stopped talking and began to sing. Kelly did the same.

A short time later, the preacher gave his message from the book of Romans.

" 'And we know that all things work together for good to them that love God, to them who are the called according to his purpose,' " Reverend Nelson read in his booming voice.

Kelly's Chance

"All things. . . . For them that love God and are called according to His purpose." Kelly was sure that meant her. The preacher was saying all things in her life would work together for good because she loved God. Surely He wanted to give her good things. The question was, would those good things be what she'd been praying for?

Kelly hadn't realized the service was over until Sarah touched her arm. "You gonna sit there all day, or did ya plan to go speak to that storekeeper who hasn't taken his eyes off you since we sat down?"

Kelly wrinkled her nose. "You're makin' that up."

"Am not." Sarah stood up. "I'd better get back to the boat and check on little Sam. Got any messages you want me to give the folks?"

Kelly got to her feet as well. "What makes you think I'm not returnin' to the boat with you?"

"Call it a hunch." Sarah bent down and grabbed the blanket. She gave it a good shake, then folded it and tucked it under Kelly's arm.

"Should I tell Mama you won't be joinin' us for the noon meal?"

Kelly felt her face heat up. Was Sarah able to read her mind these days?

"Well, I. . .uh. . .thought I might speak to Mike about my paintings. See if any more have sold."

"And if he invites you to join him for lunch?"

Kelly chewed on her lower lip. "You think I should say yes?"

Sarah swatted Kelly's arm playfully. "Of course, silly."

"What about the folks? Shouldn't I check with them first?"

"Leave that up to me."

"Okay, then. If I don't return to the boat in the next half hour, you can figure I'm havin' a picnic lunch with Mike. He did mention wantin' to do that the last time we talked."

Sarah gave Kelly a quick hug, hoisted her long skirt, and trudged off in the direction of the boat. Kelly turned toward the spot where

Mike had been sitting, but disappointment flooded her soul when she realized he was gone. With a deep sigh, she whirled around and headed the same way Sarah had gone. There was no point in sticking around now.

Kelly had only taken a few steps when she felt someone touch her shoulder. She whirled around, and her throat closed with emotion. Mike was standing so close she could feel his warm breath on her neck. She stared up at him, her heart thumping hard like the mules' hooves plodding along the hard-packed trail.

"Kelly." Mike's voice was low and sweet.

She slid her tongue across her lower lip, feeling jittery as a june bug. "I came to hear the preaching."

"Reverend Nelson delivered a good message today, didn't he?"

Kelly nodded in response. It was hard to speak. Hard to think with him standing there watching her every move.

"Can you join me for a picnic?" Mike

asked. "It will only take me a few minutes to throw something in the picnic basket, and it's the perfect day for it, don't you think?"

"Yes, yes, it is," she replied, glad she'd found her voice again.

"Then you'll join me?"

"I'd be happy to. Is there anything I can bring?"

"Just a hearty appetite and that blanket you're holding."

Kelly glanced down at the woolen covering Sarah had tucked under her arm. Her sister must have been pretty certain Mike would be taking her on a picnic. "Where should I meet you?"

"How about at the pond by the lock tender's house? That way you won't have to worry about anyone seeing us walk there together."

Kelly knew Mike was probably referring to her dad, and he was right. It would be much better if Papa didn't know she was going on a picnic with the storekeeper.

"Okay, I'll head there now, and maybe

even get a bit of sketching done while I'm waitin' for you."

Mike winked at her. "See you soon then."

"Yes, soon."

CHAPTER 26

❖

The warmth of the sun beating down on her head and shoulders felt like healing balm as Kelly reclined on her blanket a few feet from the pond. She always enjoyed springtime, with its gentle breezes, pleasantly warm temperatures, and flowers blooming abundantly along the towpath. Summer would be here soon, and that meant hot, humid days, which made it more difficult to walk the mules. So she would enjoy each day of spring and try to be content when the sweltering days of summer came upon them.

"Are you taking a nap?"

Kelly bolted upright at the sound of Mike's voice. "I. . .uh. . .was just resting and enjoyin' the warmth of the sun."

He took a seat beside her and placed the picnic basket in the center of the blanket. "It's a beautiful Lord's Day, isn't it?"

She nodded and smiled.

"I hope you're hungry, because I packed us a big lunch."

Kelly eyed the basket curiously. "What did ya fix?"

Mike opened the lid and withdrew a loaf of bread, along with a hunk of cheese and some roast beef slices. "For sandwiches," he announced.

Kelly licked her lips as her mouth began to water. She hadn't realized how hungry she was until she saw the food.

"I also brought canned peaches, a bottle of goat's milk, and a chocolate cake for dessert."

"Where did you get all this?" Surely the man hadn't baked the cake and bread, canned the peaches, and milked a goat. When would he have had the time? Papa always said cooking and baking were women's work, although he had been forced to do some of it when Mama had taken sick last year.

Mike fingered his mustache as a smile spread across his face. "I must confess, I bought the bread and cake from Mrs. Harris, the wife of one of our lock tenders living along the canals. I often buy her baked goods and sell them in my store. The peaches came from Mrs. Wilson, who lives in Walnutport."

"And the goat's milk?"

He wiggled his eyebrows. "I recently traded one of my customers a couple of kerosene lamps for the goat."

"Couldn't they have paid for the lamps, or were you actually wantin' a goat?"

He chuckled. "Truth of the matter, they didn't have any cash, and even though I offered them credit, they preferred to do a bit of bartering." He poured some of the goat's milk into a cup and handed it to Kelly. "I enjoy animals, so Henrietta is a nice addition to the little barnyard family I adopted this winter."

"Your barnyard family? How many other animals do you have?"

"Besides Blaze, my horse, and Henrietta the goat, I also own a cat, a dozen chickens, and I'm thinking about getting a pig or two."

Kelly shook her head. "Sounds like a lot of work to me."

"Maybe so, but a man can get lonely living all by himself, and taking care of the critters gives me something to do when I'm not minding the store."

Kelly was about to take a sip of her goat's milk, when Mike took hold of her hand. "Shall we pray?"

"Of course."

After Mike's simple prayer, he sliced the bread and handed Kelly a plate with a hunk of cheese, some meat, and two thick pieces of bread. She made quick work out of eating it, savoring every bite.

When they finished their sandwiches, Mike opened the jar of peaches and placed two chunks on each of their plates.

"Don't you ever get lonely walking the towpath by yourself?"

"I'm not really alone," Kelly replied. "Herman and Hector are good company, and of course now that Sarah's back, she sometimes walks with me."

His eyebrows drew together. "Mind if I ask where Sarah's husband is?"

Kelly felt her stomach tighten. She didn't want to think of the way Sam had run off and left his family, much less talk about it.

"I guess it's none of my business," Mike said, before she could make a reply. "Forget I even asked."

Kelly reached out and touched the sleeve of his shirt. "It's all right. Others will no doubt be askin', so I may as well start by telling you the facts." She swallowed hard, searching for the right words. "Shortly after we arrived in Easton, I ran into my sister at the Simon Silk Mill, where I'd gone looking for a job."

Mike nodded.

"Sarah told me Sam had lost his job at Warren Soapstone. Said it was because he'd gotten mad at his boss and talked back." Kelly paused a moment and was surprised when Mike reached for her hand. She didn't pull it away. His hand was warm and comforting.

"Sarah said Sam had been staying home with the baby while she worked," Kelly continued. "I invited her to drop by the boarding-house where we were staying, so Mama and me could meet Sam Jr."

"And did she stop by?" Mike asked.

"Yes, the next Saturday. But as soon as I laid eyes on her, I knew somethin' was wrong."

"What happened?"

"She said Sam up and left her, which meant she had no one to watch the baby." Kelly's eyes filled with tears, just thinking about how terribly her sister had been treated. "I agreed to move in with Sarah and watch the little guy while she was at work."

"So that's how you were able to get so many paintings done." Mike squeezed Kelly's hand. "That was a fine thing you did, agreeing to help care for your sister's child." He frowned. "I'm sorry to hear Sam Turner couldn't face up to his responsibilities. Guess maybe he wasn't ready to be a husband or father."

Kelly snorted. "I'd say most men aren't ready."

"That's not true," Mike said, shaking his head. "I'm more than ready. Have been for a couple of years." He eyed Kelly in a curious sort of way. What was he thinking? Why was he smiling at her like that?

She didn't know what to say, so she withdrew her hand and popped a hunk of peach into her mouth.

"Ever since my folks passed away, I've felt an emptiness in my heart," Mike went on to say. "And after Alvin and John left home to start up their fishin' business in New Jersey, I've had a hankering for a wife and a houseful of kids." He stared down at his plate. "I've been praying for some time that God would give me a Christian wife, and later some children who'd take over the store someday." His gaze lifted to her face, and she swallowed hard. "I feel confident that God has answered my prayer and sent the perfect woman for my needs."

Kelly's heart began to pound. Surely Mike couldn't mean her. He must be referring to someone else. . .maybe Betsy Nelson, the preacher's daughter. It was obvious that the woman had eyes for Mike. Maybe the two of them had begun courting while Kelly was away for the winter months.

"I think the preacher's daughter would make any man a fine wife," Kelly mumbled.

"The preacher's daughter?" Mike's furrowed brows showed his obvious confusion.

"Betsy Nelson. I believe she likes you."

Mike set his plate on the blanket, then

took hold of Kelly's and did the same with it. He leaned forward, placed his hands on her shoulders, and kissed her lips so tenderly she thought she might swoon. When the kiss ended, he whispered, "It's you I plan to marry, and it has been all along."

Kelly's mouth dropped open, but before she could find her voice, he spoke again. "Ever since that day you and your folks came into my store so you could buy a pair of boots, I've been interested in you. I thought you might feel the same."

"I. . .I. . .," she sputtered.

"We can be married by Preacher Nelson whenever you feel ready," Mike continued, as though the matter was entirely settled. "I'm hoping we can start a family right away, and—"

Kelly jumped up so quickly she knocked over the jar still half-full of peaches. "I won't be anyone's wife!" she shouted. "Especially not someone who only wants a woman so he can have children he can put to work and never pay!"

Mike scrambled to his feet, but before he had a chance to say one word, she turned on her heel and bounded away, not caring that she'd left her blanket behind.

Mike stood staring at Kelly's retreating form and feeling like his breath had been snatched away. What had gone wrong? What had he said to upset her so?

Taking in a deep breath of air, Mike tried to sort out his tangled emotions. Kelly had to be the one for him. After all, she'd appeared at his store last year only moments after his prayer for a wife. He'd thought they'd been drawing closer each time they spent alone. She'd allowed him to kiss her. Had Kelly really believed he was interested in Betsy Nelson? And what had she meant by shouting that she didn't want to be anyone's wife—especially not someone who wanted a woman so he could have children he could put to work and never pay?

"I would never do such a thing," Mike

muttered. "I can't imagine why she would think so, either."

An image of Amos McGregor popped into Mike's mind. The man was a tyrant, and he remembered Kelly saying on several occasions that her dad had refused to pay her any money for leading the mules. That was the reason her sister, Sarah, had run off with Sam Turner a couple years ago.

Mike slapped the side of his head and moaned. "How could I have been so stupid and insensitive? I should have realized Kelly might misunderstand my intentions."

He closed his eyes and lifted his face toward the sky. "Father in heaven, please guide me. I love Kelly, and I thought by her actions she might have come to love me. Help me convince her, Lord."

Chapter 27

Kelly knew her face must be red and tear-stained. Her parents would want to know where she'd gone after the church service, but she couldn't face anyone now or answer any questions. She just wanted to be alone in her room, to cry and sort out her feelings.

Kelly climbed onto the boat and hurried to her bedroom, relieved that nobody was in sight. They were probably all taking naps. She flung the door of her room open and flopped onto the bed, hoping she, too, might be able to nap. But sleep eluded her as she thought about the things that had transpired on her picnic with Mike.

Did the man really expect her to marry him and bear his children, just so they could work in his store? Mike hadn't really said it would be without pay, but then she'd run off so fast there hadn't been a chance for him to say anything more. Maybe she should have asked him to explain his intentions. Maybe she should have admitted that she'd come to care for him in a special way.

A fresh set of tears coursed down Kelly's cheeks, and she sniffed deeply while she swiped at them with the back of her hand. *I can never tell Mike how he makes me feel. If I did, he would think I wanted to get married and raise his children. I won't marry a man just to get away from Papa's mean temper or the hard work I'm expected to do. I want the opportunity to support myself. I need the chance to prove I can make money of my own.*

She squeezed her eyes shut. "Dear God, please show me what to do. Help me learn to be content with my life, and help me forget how much I enjoyed Mike's kiss."

For the next several weeks, Kelly avoided Mike's store. Even when they stopped for supplies, she stayed outside with the mules. She couldn't face Mike. He probably thought she was an idiot for running out on their picnic, and it was too difficult for her to explain the way she'd been thinking. She was pretty sure she loved him, but she couldn't give in to her feelings. No way did she want to end up like Mama, who had to endure Papa's harsh tongue and controlling ways. Nor did Kelly wish to be like her sister, raising a baby alone and continuing to work for their father with no pay.

Today was hotter than usual, especially since it was only the end of May. Kelly looked longingly at the canal as she plodded along the towpath, wishing she could stop and take a dip in the cooling waters. Even though she was leery of water moccasins, Kelly would have set her fears aside and gone swimming if they'd stopped for any length of time.

A short time later, Kelly's wish was granted. A long line of boats waited at the lock just a short way past Mike's store. No telling how long they might be held up. Kelly decided she would take off her boots and go wading. No point in getting her whole body wet when all she needed was a bit of chilly water on her legs to get cooled off.

She made sure both mules had been given a drink of water, then secured them to a nearby tree. She thought about asking Sarah to join her in the water, but the baby was down for a nap, and Sarah and Mama had taken advantage of the stop and begun washing clothes.

Kelly plunked herself on the ground, slipped off her boots and socks, and stood up. It was time to get cooled off.

Mike closed the door behind a group of tourists from New York who were traveling by boat up the canal. They'd dropped by his store in search of food supplies, but to his surprise, they'd been favorably impressed with Kelly's artwork. So much so that Mike had sold all of Kelly's paintings, and two of the travelers had asked if he would be getting any more, saying they would stop by the store on their return trip.

Mike promised to try to get more, but after the customers left, he wondered how it would be possible. He hadn't seen Kelly since their picnic, when he'd been dumb enough to announce that he wanted to make her his wife. Her folks had stopped by a couple of times, but Kelly never came inside.

He'd been tempted to seek her out, but after a time of prayer, Mike decided to leave their relationship in God's hands. He had tried to take control of the matter before, and it only left him with an ache in his heart. From now on, he'd let God decide if Kelly McGregor was meant for him. If she showed an interest, he would know she was the one. If not, then he needed to move on with his life. Maybe he wasn't meant to have a wife.

Feeling a headache coming on, Mike closed his store a bit early and went outside for some air. Even though he had never learned to swim well and couldn't do much more than dive in the water and paddle back to the lock, today seemed like the perfect day for getting wet. Wearing only a pair of trousers he'd rolled up to the knees, Mike jumped into the canal near the stop gate.

With her skirt held up, Kelly plodded back and forth along the bank by the lock tender's house. Several swimmers had been there earlier, but most had gone for the day. It would be awhile until Papa was ready to go, as there had been a break in the lock and all the boats were still held up. Kelly decided to take advantage of this free time to get some sketching done. She'd left her drawing tablet on the grass next to her boots and was about to reclaim it when she noticed Mike Cooper in the water. He dove from one dock, then crossed the gates and grabbed hold of the dock on the other side. She was surprised to see him, as she remembered Mike saying once that he wasn't a good swimmer and didn't go into the canal very often.

Kelly stood still, watching in fascination as Mike took another dive. She waited for him to resurface on the other side, but he didn't come up where he should have.

A sense of alarm shot through her body when she noticed small bubbles on top of the water. They seemed to be coming from a large roll of moss about ten feet above the gates. With no thought for her own safety, Kelly jerked off her skirt, and wearing only her white pantalets and cotton blouse, she dove into the water and swam toward the spot where she'd seen the bubbles. Her scream echoed over the water. "Hold on, Mike! I'm comin'!"

A few seconds later, Kelly dove under the water and spotted Mike, thrashing about while he tried to free his hands and feet from the twisted moss. Visions of them both being drowned flashed through her mind as Kelly tried to untangle the mess. Mike wouldn't hold still. He was obviously in a state of panic. At one point, he grabbed Kelly around the neck, nearly choking her to death.

Her lungs began to burn, and she knew she needed air quickly. Desperation surged within. Her insides felt as if they would burst. She sent up a prayer and did the only thing that came to mind.

Pop! Kelly smacked Mike right in the nose. Blood shot out in every direction, but Mike loosened his grip on her neck. Using all her strength and inner resolve, Kelly managed to get his hands and feet free from the moss, and she kicked her way to the surface, pulling Mike along.

When Mike's face cleared the water, she breathed a sigh of relief. Gasping for breath, Kelly propelled them through the murky water until at last they were both on the shore. Mike lay there, white as a sheet, and Kelly worried that he might be dead. She rolled him over and began to push down on his back. A short time later, he started coughing and sputtering.

A great sense of relief flooded Kelly's soul. She grabbed hold of the skirt she'd left on the grass, ripped off a piece, and held it against Mike's bleeding nose. How close she'd come to losing the man she loved. The realization sent shivers up Kelly's spine, and she trembled and let out a little sob.

Mike opened his eyes and stared up at her, a look of confusion on his face. "What happened? Where am I?"

"You were trapped in a wad of moss," she rasped. "I'm awful sorry, but I had to punch you in the nose to get you to stop fightin'."

He blinked several times. "You hit me?"

She nodded. "Sorry, but I didn't know what else to do."

Mike reached up and touched her hand where she held the piece of material against his nose. "Is it broken?"

She pulled the cloth back and studied the damage. "I don't think so. The bleedin' seems to be almost stopped."

"You saved my life."

"I guess I did, but it was God who gave me the strength to do it."

He clutched her hand. "Why would you do that if you don't care about me?"

She frowned. "Who says I don't care?"

"Do you?" Mike's eyes were seeking, his voice imploring her to tell the truth.

Kelly's heart was beating so hard she thought it might burst wide open. She'd been fighting her feelings for Mike all these months, yet seeing him almost drown made her realize she wouldn't know what to do if he wasn't part of her life. Was love enough? If she were to marry Mike, would he expect her and their children to work for free at his store?

"Kelly, my love," Mike murmured. "You're the answer to my prayers."

"You were prayin' someone would find you in the moss and save your life?"

He laughed, coughed, and tried to sit up.

"You'd better lie still a few more minutes," she instructed. "That was quite an ordeal you came through."

"I'm okay," he insisted as he pulled himself to a sitting position in front of her.

"Are you sure?"

"I'm sure about one thing."

"What's that?"

He pulled her into his arms. "I'm sure I love you, and I believe God brought us together. Will you marry me, Kelly McGregor?"

Before Kelly could answer, Mike leaned over and kissed her upturned mouth. When the kiss was over, he said, "I promise never to treat you harshly, and I won't ask you or any children we may be blessed with to work for free. If you help me run the store, you'll earn half the money, same as me. If our kids help out, they'll get paid something, too."

She opened her mouth, but he cut her off. "There's more."

"More?" she echoed.

He nodded. "This morning, a group of tourists came by the store, and they bought the rest of your paintings."

"All of them?"

"Yes, and they said they'd be stopping by the store on their return trip to New York, so if you have any more pictures, they'll probably buy those as well."

Kelly could hardly believe it. All her pictures sold? It was too much to digest at once. And Mike asking her to be his wife and help run the store, agreeing to give her half of what they made? She pinched herself on the arm.

"What are you doing?" Mike asked with a little scowl.

"Makin' sure I'm not dreaming."

He kissed her again. "Does this feel like a dream?"

She nodded and giggled. "It sure does."

"Kelly, I've been thinking that I could add on to the store. Make a sort of gallery for you to paint and display your pictures. Maybe you could sell some art supplies to customers, as well."

Her mouth fell open. She'd been dreaming about an art gallery for such a long time, and it didn't seem possible that her dream could be realized if she married Mike. "I'd love to have my own art gallery," she murmured, "but I won't marry you for that reason."

"You won't? Does that mean you don't love me?"

Mike's dejected expression was almost her undoing, and Kelly placed both her hands on his bare shoulders. "I do love you, and I will marry you, but not because of the promise of a gallery."

"What then?"

"I'll agree to become your wife for one reason and only one." Kelly leaned over and gently kissed the tip of Mike's nose. "I love you,

Mike Cooper—with all my heart and soul. This is finally my chance for real happiness, and I'm not about to let it go."

Mike looked up and closed his eyes. "Thank You, Lord, for such a special woman."

EPILOGUE

———— ❀ ————

It was a pleasant morning on the last Saturday of September. So much had happened in the last four months that Kelly could hardly believe it. From her spot in front of an easel, she glanced across the room where her husband of three months stood waiting on a customer.

Mike must have guessed Kelly was watching him, for he looked over at her and winked.

She smiled and lifted her hand in response.

Being married to Mike was better than she ever could have imagined. Not only was he a kind, Christian man, but he'd been true to his word and had added on to the store so Kelly could have her art gallery. Whenever she wasn't helping him in the store, she painted pictures, always adding a verse of scripture above her signature. This was Kelly's way of telling others about God, who had been so good to her and the family.

Sam Turner had returned to the canal a few weeks ago, apologizing to Sarah and begging her to give him the chance to prove his love for her. Rather than going back to the city, the couple and the baby were living with Sam's parents. Sam assisted his dad with the lock chores, and Sarah helped her mother-in-law make bread and other baked goods, which they sold to many of the boaters who came through. They'd also begun to take in some washing, since many of the boatmen were either single or didn't bring their wives along to care for that need.

Kelly's Chance

Kelly had finally seen the seashore along the coast of New Jersey, where Mike's brothers lived. They'd gone there for their honeymoon, and she'd been able to meet Alvin, John, and their wives.

The most surprising thing that had happened in the last few months was the change that had come over Kelly's dad. He'd accepted one of Reverend Nelson's cards with a Bible verse written on it, and Papa's heart was beginning to change. Not only was he no longer so ill-tempered, but Papa had given money to Kelly and Sarah, saying they'd both worked hard and deserved it. Since neither of them was available to work for him any longer, he'd willingly hired two young men—one to drive the mules, the other to help steer the boat. Kelly figured if she kept praying, in time Papa would turn his life completely over to the Lord.

When the front door opened and Betsy Nelson walked in, Kelly smiled and waved. What had happened in the life of the preacher's daughter was the biggest surprise of all.

"That's a beautiful sunset you're working on," Betsy said, stepping up beside Kelly.

"Thanks. Would ya like to have it?"

Betsy shook her head. "I'm afraid where I'm going there will be no use for pretty pictures."

Kelly nodded, knowing Betsy was talking about South America, where she'd recently decided to go as a missionary. "No, I suppose not."

"I'm leaving tomorrow morning for Easton, and then I'll ride the train to New York. From there, I'll board a boat for South America," Betsy said.

"Everyone will miss your zither playin' on Sunday mornings," Kelly commented.

Betsy gave her a quick hug. "Thanks, but I'll be back someday, and when I return, I expect you and Mike will have a whole houseful of little ones."

Kelly smiled and placed one hand against her stomach. In about seven months the first of the Cooper children would make an appearance, and she couldn't wait to become a mother. God had given her a wonderful Christian man to share the rest of her life with, and she knew he would be an amazing father.

As soon as Betsy and the other customer left, Mike moved across the room and took Kelly into his arms. "I sure love you, Mrs. Cooper."

"And I love you," she murmured against his chest.

Mike bent his head to capture her lips, and Kelly thanked the Lord for giving her the chance to find such happiness. She could hardly wait to see what the future held for Cooper's General Store on the Lehigh Canal.

RECIPE FOR HUNKS-A-GO PUDDING

Make a batter with the following ingredients:

> 1 cup flour
> 1 tsp. salt
> 1 cup milk
> 2 eggs

Pour the batter into hot grease left over from cooked roast beef. Cover with a lid and cook on top of the stove until done.

DISCUSSION QUESTIONS

1. During the canal era, many young men and women were forced to work for their parents with no pay, so they often married young in order to get away. What would you say to someone who wanted to get married just so they could leave home?

2. Kelly didn't like leading the mules that pulled her father's canal boat. She prayed that God would fulfill her dream of getting away from the canal and opening her own art gallery. Since that was her only goal, she shied away from love and romance. Have you ever had such determination to reach a goal that you didn't see other possibilities?

3. One of the reasons Kelly was against marriage was because her father was so harsh with her and her mother. What are some ways we can move past the

things that happened to us during our childhood?

4. Most of the time Kelly preferred to be alone. Being around the people in town made her feel nervous and self-conscious. What are some ways a shy person might overcome their self-consciousness? How can we help someone who's shy and has no self-esteem?

5. As a new Christian, Kelly knew her negative attitude about certain things was wrong. The resentment Kelly harbored toward her father kept her from worshiping God as she should. Has there ever been a time in your life when you let resentments interfere with your walk with Lord? What steps can we take to work through our resentments?

6. Kelly was envious of Betsy Nelson, the preacher's daughter, who had fine clothes

and good manners. Have you ever struggled with jealousy? What does God's Word tell us about being envious of others? How can we deal with jealousy?

7. Kelly's father had no appreciation for her artistic talent and often ridiculed her for the drawings she did. How can a child rise above ridicule from their parents? What are some ways we can encourage others to make use of their talents, despite negative comments that have been made by their parents?

8. Mike wanted nothing more than to find a good woman and get married. When he met Kelly, he felt that she was the one. But Kelly seemed to be holding back, and he felt sure he'd pushed her away when she moved to the city. Have you ever been in a relationship where you felt you had pushed too hard? Perhaps it was the other person who'd done the pushing. What's

the best way to deal with someone who doesn't seem ready for a close relationship? Is there ever a time when it's right to push ourselves on someone in order to make them our friend?

9. When Betsy Nelson let it be known that she was interested in Mike, he tried to be nice without leading her on. However, on more than one occasion, Betsy took Mike's politeness to mean that he had an interest in her. Would there have been a better way for Mike to have handled things with Betsy?

ABOUT THE AUTHOR

Wanda E. Brunstetter is a bestselling author who enjoys writing historical, as well as Amish-themed novels. Wanda's interest in the Lehigh Canal began when she married her husband, Richard, who grew up in Pennsylvania, near the canal. Wanda and Richard have made numerous trips to Pennsylvania, where they have several friends and relatives. They've walked the towpath, ridden on a canal boat, and toured the lock tender's house. Wanda hopes her readers will enjoy this historical series as much as she enjoyed researching and writing it.

Wanda and her husband have two grown children, six grandchildren and one great-grandchild. In her spare time, Wanda enjoys photography, ventriloquism, gardening, reading, stamping, and having fun with her family.

In addition to her novels, Wanda has written two Amish cookbooks, an Amish devotional, several Amish children's books, as well as many novellas, stories, articles, poems, and puppet scripts.

Visit Wanda's website at www.wandabrunstetter.com.

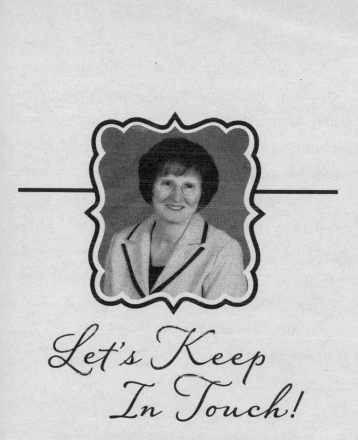

Let's Keep In Touch!

Want to know what Wanda's up to and be the first to hear about new releases, specials, the latest news, and more? Like Wanda on Facebook!

 Visit facebook.com/WandaBrunstetterFans today!